WHIPPED

WHIPPED

Alex Lux

DARING
BOOKS

AlexLuxBooks.com

Copyright © 2015 Alex Lux
Cover Art Copyright © 2014 Dmytry Karpov

ISBN-10: 1939559340
ISBN-13: 9781939559340

Published by Daring Books

Edited by Anne Chaconas

To Anne for cracking her whip
And keeping us going

TABLE OF CONTENTS

ONE

Vi

I pull a black 14" dildo from the box at my feet and place it front and center on the table, moving tubes of lube, a set of handcuffs and an assortment of butt plugs to the side. "I've got a feeling we're going to sell this bad boy today," I say to Zoe, who's checking our front window display.

When she laughs it's like perfectly pitched bells ringing. Like what Tinker Bell might sound like in a mostly full-grown adult body. I say 'mostly' because my business partner and friend struggles to hit 5' even in heels.

She practically skips over, her vibrant purple lips matching her pixie hair, smiling widely. "Looks great. I will be very impressed with the woman—or man—who goes home with that."

"You and me both!" I check the clock, a red retro thing we found at an estate sale. "Time to open."

Whipped is our baby. After some minor ennui on my part with my job as a full-time Dominatrix, I realized I was ready for a new challenge, and the timing was perfect for Zoe and me to create an intimate, fun, trendy and educational adult toy store in a town that can never have too much adult fun.

If you can't sell a dildo in Vegas, you're doing it wrong.

Our instincts proved true and six months in, business is booming. Unfortunately, stocking a store with the best products isn't cheap. We both emptied our savings into Whipped, and while we know we'll eventually break out of the red, we have to eke by until then.

As if reading my mind, Zoe hands me a stack of mail. I shuffle through it, frowning. "More bills. Must our vendors always insist on getting paid? It's uncharitable," I say in a mock southern accent, dramatically sweeping my red hair off my shoulder and channeling my best Scarlett O'Hara.

Zoe taps her metallic purple nails on the counter. "It truly is. You'd think having the privilege of selling to sexy, adorable, brilliant women such as ourselves would be enough. What has the world come to?"

I grin and wink at her as I drop the demanding envelopes into a file behind our register. "We'll figure it out."

She nods. "I know. In the meantime, how's the hunt for a roommate coming?"

At the reminder I check my phone and see another email from "Inferno12." I laugh at a lame joke involving clowns he sent and confirm our meeting for tonight. "I might have found someone," I say. "I haven't met him yet, but he seems nice and we get along online. I'll know by tomorrow, though at this point I'd likely rent to the evil clown from *American Horror Story* to get Mr. Harris off my back."

She pats my hand sympathetically. "Another person who insists on being paid what they're owed?"

I laugh. "It's outrageous."

The bell above our door rings and Zoe disappears into the back to finish inventory while I smile warmly at the grandmotherly woman shyly looking around. I give her space and take a moment to gauge what she thinks she's here for, and what she's actually here for. There's usually a difference, even if the customer doesn't yet know it.

She's in her 70s, I'd guess, with short, halo-like, white permed hair and a pastel pantsuit paired with a floral blouse. She clutches her beige purse against her stomach like she's not sure why she came in, but I see her eyes light up as she looks around. I'm guessing she's either recently widowed and ready to explore her own sexuality, or she's in a new relationship. She's mostly looking at our books, but I see her eyes flicker to the center display I just set up.

I walk over to her, my body language relaxed, warm, open. "Hello. I'm Vi, co-owner here. Is there anything I can help you find?"

"Thank you, young lady. I…well, I guess I have some things I want to try while I'm still around and kickin'. And I heard lovely things about your store."

I send a heartfelt thank you to whoever talked us up as I smile at her. "Are you looking for something for yourself or for you and a partner?" I gently guide her around the store as we talk, gauging how she responds to the different toys, creams, lotions and lingerie on display.

"Just for me. My husband died about a year ago, and I've been feeling this…itch? Does that make sense?"

I rest a hand on her arm. "Of course it does. It's completely natural and healthy to want to express your sexuality and enjoy it."

Her smile widens. "That's what I think too," she says. Then she cups her hand over her mouth and leans in, as if telling me a great secret. "I do think I shocked my Bridge Club when I told them I'd be coming here. But just watch, they'll be following in my footsteps soon enough, the old birds!"

I couldn't help but share in her laughter as she relaxed in the knowledge that she would get no judgment from me. She reached for a small vibrator—the Silver Bullet—and held it up. "Maybe this?"

I hold her eyes for a moment. "That's a good brand, and it works well. But..." I flick my eyes to the 14" beauty behind her. She turns and looks at it, her eyes widening as I point. "I think that's what you really want."

I can see her internal battle as she tries to decide if she should give in to her own cravings. I make it easier, taking both the bullet and the dildo and walking to the counter. "Tell you what," I propose, still smiling. "Get the dildo, and I'll throw in the vibrator as a gift. That way, if you don't like it, you'll still have something else to try."

She follows me to the register and stands opposite me, her purse already open, a secret smile on her lips. "I suppose it couldn't hurt to try."

I wink at her. "I promise, you won't regret it."

As she pays, I place her new toys in a bag with a few of our cards and hand it to her. "It's been nice talking with you. I threw in some coupons for your Bridge Club, should they be so inclined to follow in your steps."

I can still hear her laughing as she leaves the shop, the golden bell heralding her departure.

Zoe joins me at the register, a look of awe on her face, not for me, but for the woman who just left our store. "Mad props to her. I hope when I'm her age I'm still that adventurous."

I look down at my petite partner with affection. "I have no doubt you will be."

Zoe's phone beeps and she checks it, then types in a text as she bites her lower lip and furrows her carefully plucked brows.

"Boyfriend trouble again?" I ask, knowing the signs all too well.

She looks up, all the joy sucked from her expression by this one text. "He's on his 'no sex until marriage' kick again. His priest convinced him I'm causing him to sin so now he wants to sleep in separate rooms."

"It'll last three days at most," I say.

"I know. But in the meantime, it sucks. And not just the no sex. But the guilt, the pressure, the way he makes me feel like the whore of Babylon, even though he's the one who initiated our first time two years ago, and he's the one who asked me to move in with him. This man is just thoroughly confused."

"That's *one* word for it." My sarcasm is too thick to hide and she flinches.

"He's a good man. Kind, nice, respectful. He just has some religious hangups. No one's perfect." Her huge blue anime eyes look sad, and I put my arm around her shoulders and side hug her.

"I know he's not a bad guy. I just want you to be happy, in and out of the bedroom. A guy who has to shower immediately after sex each and every time isn't going to work long term for a girl who owns a sex toy shop. Especially since he's still never even been here and insists on telling people you work at the mall."

I drop my arm and she paces the shop, fixing displays that don't need fixing. "When you say it like that, it sounds awful."

That's because it *is* awful, but I've said enough. Zoe is the sweetest person you'll ever meet. Not a mean bone in her tiny body. I'm fiercely protective of her, but I often have to remind myself she's also a grown woman who can make her own choices. Even when it comes to Henry.

"What about you?" she says, oh-so-subtly dodging the conversation about her love life and instead focusing on mine. "It's been almost a year since your breakup with Chad. Any new men on the horizon?"

"Only the occasional sub I've hooked up with at the club," I say, as *I* now straighten merchandise that doesn't need straightening. "But nothing serious. I'm too focused on our business to think about that right now." I had the perfect guy in Chad: smart, sexy, charming, talented, a committed submissive who enjoyed my Dominatrix side...but once I got everything I always thought I wanted, it didn't work. And I haven't been ready for a new commitment since.

When the bell rings, signaling another customer, we both turn with smiles which turn to adolescent giggles when we see who it is. "He's back!" Zoe says.

He is indeed, in all his ripped glory. The man in question struts through our store with a new blonde on his arm. He's dressed in jeans that hang at his hips 'in just that way,' to lamely quote every romance novel ever written. And that's all he wears. Seriously, dude never has a fucking shirt on. Not once, and he's come in at least once a week since we opened. Always with a different girl, always with the jeans and no shirt, always with the cash—and always with the sexy.

Oh, and did I mention he's Australian? Because he is. Not that it matters. I can't stand the guy. I don't care that his abs are made of steel or that he looks like he's hung like a horse. I blithely ignore his deep tan, perfect white teeth and eyes the shade of the bluest ocean. I won't even think about his bed-head hair that's always that flawless mess of dark blond that looks like he's been running his hands through it.

No, none of that matters. He's the epitome of player. He's the reason I'm seriously considering a sign that says "No shirt, no shoes, no service." Except he spends a lot of money here and we need customers like him, as Zoe reminds me every week.

The Aussie Hottie browses through our displays, picking, as always, the best of everything. The woman with him drapes her body against him as if she might die if they aren't touching at all times. Without any shame she rubs his cock up and down over his jeans and nibbles on his ear. Worried they might actually have sex in my store at any moment, I smile and walk over to them. "How can I help you today?"

He nods to the girl who giggles and wiggles off to look around. "Oh, just the usual today. Unless you have something new and exciting for me?"

The way he asks that, I feel like he's hinting at more than just our products, but I ignore the double entendre and shake my head. "Just what you see here. I don't think we've had any new deliveries since your last visit here with…" I cock my head, pretending to forget the other woman's name, even though I never knew it.

He smiles, a dimple forming on his cheek. "That was Natalie." He glances at the blonde. "That's Jessie."

"You're a busy man," I say. I'm not really judging. One of my best friends is a total player, too. Always a different girl. But he's also up front and honest. I don't know if this guy is or not.

"It's a distraction. For me and for them," he says, his eyes digging into mine as if trying to uncover my secrets.

"Do they know that?"

"Sure they do." He steps closer, our bodies inches apart. So close I can smell his aftershave. Minty spice. "And they're open for more than just a one-on-one, if you're ever interested."

Not that I haven't ever experimented with a threesome, but I've generally found they're better in theory than in reality. Still, it's been awhile since even a casual sexual experience for me, and my body feels the heat of him even as my mind tells me to walk away. Nothing good can come from a man this confident, this clearly used to being in control. Not my type. At. All.

I take his purchases to the register as he pulls out his cash.

"Why new toys every week?" I ask, handing him the bag.

"I may be a *coit*," he says, his accent stronger with the slang that I assume is Australian for 'I sleep with *all the women,*' "but I'm not a cheap asshole. And I don't reuse sex toys with different women. I let them keep whatever we use together."

A begrudging respect grows for him, but his cockiness still rubs me the wrong way.

He hands me a small stack of gold embossed cards with VIP written on them. "If you and your friend ever want a night out, come by around 10pm Wednesday through Sunday nights and tell them the Aussie Hottie sent you. I'll make sure you get good seats."

He winks at me as he walks out the door with his date by his side, and my cheeks flush to what I'm sure is a bright red.

Zoe and I are both quiet until we're sure he's out of earshot, then she starts laughing. Hard. Like doubled-over-at-the-waist laughing. "I can't believe he knows our name for him!"

I can't help but follow suit and it feels good to laugh so hard your sides hurt. "He's a cheeky bastard for sure."

As our breathing comes back and our laughs slow down, Zoe nudges my shoulder. "He's sexy as sin, Vi. And he's obvs into you. You should do him."

I shake my head and shove his note into my pocket. "I am not 'doing' the Aussie Hottie. He's definitely not my type."

Zoe just grins and returns to inventory.

The rest of the day speeds by as we work with our customers to find them what they want and need. By the end of the day I'm tired, but happy and excited to meet my potential new roommate.

Even more excited when I get another passive-aggressive note from Mr. Harris.

Miss Reynolds,

If it's not too much to ask, I would greatly appreciate some indication that this month's rent might perhaps be paid before next month's rent becomes due. Though owing two months' rent would save me on paper, as I could just send these notes for both amounts owed at once. Still, if we could avoid further social embarrassment I would certainly be grateful. And I'm sure it would be easier for you to not have to wait quietly behind your door pretending not to be home when I come by to inquire about the money owed.

Sincerely,
Your landlord and neighbor,
Mr. Harris

I glance over at his side of the duplex and see that his car is gone. Good. I hurry over and jot down my response note to leave on his door.

Mr. Harris,

Thank you for your kind note and gentle understanding of my unusual position. As someone who has lived here for several years and always paid her rent on time, I'm sure you can appreciate that this is an unusual circumstance which I'm trying to mitigate in a timely manner. Your patience is always appreciated.

Sincerely,

Miss Reynolds

That done, I slink into my house before he can return. I hate owing money and being late on payments, despite my joking with Zoe. I've never been in this position before, but I know I'll get caught up soon.

My doorbell rings and I check the condo to make sure everything is in its place before going to answer it. I might be meeting my new roommate, which is why my place is unusually clean.

But when I open my door, it isn't Inferno12 standing there. It's the Aussie Hottie. This time, though, he's wearing a shirt.

His blue eyes widen when he sees me, then his face spreads into an entirely too sexy grin. "Well, isn't this a fine bit of luck!"

TWO

Lach

A thick wad will get you about anything. A thick wad of cash, that is. "Four months rent upfront. After that, I'll have my house, and you don't have to see me again. Except at your store."

I throw Vi the roll of bills, and she catches it. We've made the introductions. We now know names, but I can tell she's shocked to see me here. A part of me can't believe she's the girl I've been emailing *and* the shop owner I've been flirting with. Her eyes are wide and green and beautiful, and I can't pull my gaze from them.

She stuffs the bills somewhere...probably her pocket. I keep watching her eyes. They make me forget about the five grand. Almost. A few days ago, I wouldn't think twice about that sum. But I'm changing careers. The new one's more important, but less profitable. Non-profitable, really. Darrel calls it charity work.

Vi grits her teeth. She must be struggling with the decision to rent. I realize the fact that I've been flirting with her may not work in my favor. That's why I made my offer. Come on, wad of cash...come *on*...

She chews on her lip, pauses, then relaxes and smiles. "Deal. When do you want to move in?"

I want to say now, but she still looks shocked, so I say, "I'm ready when you are."

"I'm good whenever. Let me show you around."

The place is bigger than it looks from outside, and has a comfortable and roomy living room that opens to the kitchen and dining area. There's a giant red couch that takes up most of one wall, with a coffee table, an overstuffed chair and ottoman and a standing lamp behind it for reading.

On the kitchen table is one of those bazillion-piece puzzles with an abstract image that looks impossible to put together. She's got most of it done. "You like puzzles?"

She nods. "They relax me."

I look again at it and laugh. Because that shit does *not* look relaxing.

She leads me through a small hallway. "There's a bathroom on the right that we'll share. And *this* is your room." She opens the door to the left and I walk in.

It's a small room. The bed's a twin. There's an empty bookshelf that goes up to the ceiling and an empty dresser that goes up to my knees. It'll take some getting used to.

I drop my backpack on the floor and slide it under the bed with my foot. "I've got some stuff to do, but I'll be back tonight."

"Sure." She holds up a finger. "But, first, some rules."

"Rules?"

"Yes. No going into my room without my permission. No sitting on the right side of the couch. That side's mine. And no flirting with me."

I chuckle. "Sorry, but *no flirting* goes against my core beliefs."

"Fine, then no hooking up."

"Sorry, but—"

"No. No hooking up. If we hook up, we might break up. I'm not living with an ex."

"How about a fuckbuddy?"

She pauses, rubbing her chin. "No."

Her resistance intrigues me. It's not what I'm used to. It's fun. "Fine. I won't hook up with you. But what you decide to do—well, that's up to you."

She mocks laughter. "Ha. Ha. Don't worry. I can resist your sexy pants."

I wink. "But not what's in them. Trust me."

She blushes, then grits her teeth. Her body must be betraying her. I like having this effect. She holds her hand out. "So, do you accept the rules?"

I shake it firmly, and the blush returns to her cheeks. Women love a strong handshake. "I accept."

"Good." She shimmies out of the room, her jeans tight, and I'm glad "don't look at my ass" wasn't one of her rules. When she returns, she passes me a key. I make sure to touch her hand gently as I take it. The moment lasts longer than passing a key should. She shrugs. "Bring your stuff in whenever."

"Sure. I'll see you later." I squeeze by her, letting my palm rest on her back, and walk out of the apartment. I don't tell her all my stuff was in my backpack.

. . .

Not all of Vegas is like the Strip. There are places where the doors are falling off their hinges and the windows are full of holes. Places like the one I grew up in. Places like the one Kevin is growing up in now.

"Hey, my man Kev. How you doing?" I walk down his street, carrying a brown bag of food in my hands.

"Hey, Lach. Check this out." He smiles at me, his dark curly hair a mess, and does an ollie on his skateboard. The board is missing half its paint, and the wheels have fallen off before.

"Nice. Try pulling your knees up even higher." I step on the board and, still holding the bag of groceries, demonstrate the technique.

"Okay. I can do that." He tries again, almost going twice as high. "Thank, Lach."

We grin at each other. Kevin ran into me a few years ago. Then he attempted to run away with my wallet.

I caught him right away, and instead of calling the cops on an eleven-year-old, I found his mother. She worked double shifts, and the father had disappeared long ago. She blamed herself for the boy's slipping grades and recent criminal endeavors. I told her I wouldn't press charges, and she told me she'd get the boy straightened out. A week later, I dropped by to see how they were doing and offered them some groceries. A week after that, I dropped by again.

It's become a habit. I walk up the porch and ring the doorbell. The lock clicks, and Kevin's mother, Mary, opens the door. Her hair's all black, recently dyed. She adjusts her glasses and waves me in, a genuine smile on her broad dark face. "You know you can just come in, Lach. Family doesn't—"

"Family doesn't knock. I know."

"And you are family, my boy. Don't you forget it." She pulls me into a hug. Her hands are rough and covered in lines. Dark circles hang under her eyes. She's still searching for the beauty regime that'll make her look ten years younger.

But, the way I see it, she wears the trophies of hard work. She should be proud.

I kick my shoes off by the door and tilt my head at the brown bag at my hands. "These are for you."

"Oh, thank you, dear." She grabs the bag from me and drops it on the kitchen counter—a sad excuse for what was once some type of white linoleum but is now more yellowed than anything, but always scrubbed spotless, like everything in Mary's rundown apartment. Clean, but old and on its last leg. She ruffles through the contents. "Awww. Organic chicken. I told you not to spend the big bucks on us."

My phone buzzes. A text from Darrel. He's my manager, soon to be my old manager. I ignore it. "Can I help with dinner?"

"You've done enough for us, my boy."

I pull the bag toward me and pull out the kale and carrots. "You can repay me with the pleasure of your company."

She shakes her head, smiling. "Let me cut the carrots."

We divide up the vegetables, and I throw the chicken in the oven. Kevin runs in, skateboard in hand, half-ripped shoes on, his nose tilted up. "What's cooking?"

Wrong move, kiddo.

Mary turns on him, hands on her hips. "Kevin McAllister. What are the rules of this house?"

His shoulders droop. "No running."

Mary waves a spatula at him. "And?"

"No shoes inside." He smiles apologetically and walks back to the door, kicking off his shoes and dropping his board.

Marry lowers the Spatula of Order and Justice and mixes the green onion sauce. "Good job."

When the dinner is finished, she asks me to eat with them and, after some nagging from Kevin, I agree. The organic chicken with sauce is delicious. The company is even better. Kevin's math grade went from a C-minus to a B-plus. Mary's boss finally paid the overtime he owed her. The prick. He manages Bill's Burgers four blocks away and still insists on high-heeled waitresses. Though Mary barely mentions it, I know her feet hurt every day.

I finish my meal with a sip of green tea—Mary doesn't keep soda or alcohol in the house—and Kevin asks about my work. "You found a place for the center yet?"

I smile. "You know the Spacey Mall that closed down?"

Kevin smacks his fork down on the table. The excitement in his face reminds me of why I'm changing careers. "Oh man, that place is huge." He's right. I examined the location yesterday. It's one of those malls you could get lost in.

"I could modify it," I say. "Or maybe even tear it down and start new."

Mary's lips are tight. I call it her "holy shit" face, because she never swears. She just makes that face. "That'd be really expensive, wouldn't it?"

"It would be," I say. "But it's worth it."

"You have enough for that sort of thing?" she asks.

"Not yet."

Kevin pats her on the arm. "That's why he's getting investors, mom."

"Ah, I see." She smiles and twirls her chicken with her fork.

"I have a meeting with a few interested parties this week." If it goes well, I can finally stop counting dollars and start helping people.

My phone buzzes, and I check my texts. Darrel's asking if we're still meeting tonight. I text back yes. Might as well get it over with. I say goodbye to Kevin and Mary and jog to my BMW down the street. The sky's dark, the stars invisible. When I arrive at the Wynn, one of the finest hotels on the Strip, I hesitate at the door. This was my old home. I'd hoped to avoid it for a while.

The hotel greeter, a young man with a skillful fake smile, swings the door open for me, and I, not one to keep people waiting, stride inside. I navigate the tall hallways to the Sinatra Restaurant, barely having to watch my way. "Darrel Fowler is expecting me," I tell the staff member. He nods and escorts me to a table for two, where Darrel waits with a glass of wine. My hands are slick with sweat. I wipe them on my jeans.

"Lachlan, my friend." Darrel stands and hugs me. His voice is deep. His smile white and full of teeth. His skin is dark. People are often surprised by his Australian accent.

We sit down, and I order a chicken salad with extra vegetables. Darrel orders a barbecue steak and whispers something to the petite waitress. She giggles and saunters away. Another one-night-stand in the making. I don't judge. I know the waitress. Her name is Micky, and I had her giggling a few nights ago.

"You know I'm not coming back," I say.

His smile doesn't falter. "One more year, Lach. One more tour."

"That's what you said last tour."

He sighs, rubbing his bald head. "Because you're meant to perform. This thing you're trying to do, this..."

"Youth Center," I say. I wonder if he forgot, or just couldn't stand the words. A week ago, I asked him if he wanted to invest. He laughed and patted me on the head.

Darrel nods. "It's not you, Lach. You're meant for the stage. And besides, the guys need you."

"The guys will be fine. They've been doing this for years."

"Not without you." He frowns. He doesn't often. Darrel taught me how to dance, meet girls, spend money.

He did more than my father.

I feel my temper rising. I down my glass of ice water, and it cools me down. "I'm done." I stare into his dark eyes and see the disappointment.

He bows his head. "Two million."

"What?"

"We're prepared to offer you two million for the tour."

I can't stop myself. I laugh. "I could have used that last year."

"Last year, I knew you wouldn't leave."

Son of a bitch. I imagine punching him, something I haven't done for years, and it feels good. I want to say, "You can shove that two million up your ass," but I can't. I may need it to open the center. To help kids like Kevin.

So instead I say, "I'll think about it."

I leave my food half-eaten and pay my bill. Darrel flirts with Micky as I walk out and search for a liquor store. On the way, I scroll through my contacts. I land on Jessie. Good with her mouth. Doesn't talk a lot. She's what I need tonight. However, as I pick up a bottle of rum, my mind fixates on images of Vi. But I'm about to sleep with Jessie, so this is… hmm. Strange. The alcohol should fix that.

I grab a second bottle.

THREE

Vi

I stare at the wad of money sitting on my dresser. What the hell did I just do? I wanted a nice, respectful, quiet roommate. Someone who wouldn't intrude on my life too much. Not the womanizing ass who frequents my sex shop.

I count the money again, just to make sure it's real. It is. And this pile of cash is the answer to my question. At least it's temporary. He'll only be here a few months, just long enough for Zoe and me to get our shop in the green and to recover from our initial investment. How bad can it be?

Famous last words, right?

But I ignore my own trepidation and grab the cash before it disappears. He paid more than twice what I asked, and all up front. My landlord will be happy.

I shove rent money into an envelope and pen a quick note, then sneak out of my condo to stick it into the mail slot next door. At least now I can start entering and exiting my house without fear of confrontation.

I check the time on my cell and grab my purse. I'll have just long enough to get to the bank and keep my utilities on, if

I hurry. With a last glance at my unusually clean condo I lock up and head out.

On the drive to the bank I consider what it will mean to have a roommate. I haven't lived with anyone since I moved out of my parents' house—aside from a very brief stint with Chad, which obviously didn't end well. Even in college I scored a private dorm room. As an only child, it suited me. I guess I was going to have to learn to share my toys.

This ought to be interesting.

I make the bank just in time to get cashier's checks drawn up and taken in person to three different buildings to keep my life from being shut off.

And I still have money left. I feel like splurging but resist the urge. Instead, I set my course for home, ready to curl up with a good book and glass of wine, when my phone rings.

"Vi, hey, I need a huge favor."

"What's up, Zoe?"

"The vendor delivering our new shipment of dildos just got to the store, and I know it's my night to do receiving but Henry and I are in the middle of another…discussion, and I can't leave now. Can you cover for me? I'll close for you for a week if you do. Pretty please with cherries and extra rich whipped cream?"

I can't help but laugh, even though I feel bad for her right now and have to bite my tongue to keep from telling her to leave the ass she's with. He so does not deserve her. "Sure, I got you covered, no problem."

I hear Henry in the background…crying. *God.*

She sighs. "I gotta go…. Wait, oh shit, how did things go with the roomie? You all set?"

"Girlfriend, you are not going to believe what went down tonight."

Henry calls out to Zoe, a sound of desperation through tears and snot. She sighs again. "You've got me intrigued. I can't wait to hear every detail," she says, adding, "tomorrow?"

"Sure, tomorrow. I hope things settle down for you. If you need me, I'm here." I hang up, turn my car around and drive to Whipped.

The delivery guy is waiting there, stacks of boxes by his feet, when I arrive. I smile big and thank him for his patience.

"No worries. Where do you want them?" The guy is actually pretty sexy. A cross between a younger Brad Pitt and a current Channing Tatum.

I unlock the store and direct him toward the back, where we keep our inventory. "Could you stack them here?"

I can't help but put an extra sway to my hips as I walk, and I see him noticing my ass, which pleases me.

And I know he sees me noticing his bulging muscles under his FedEx uniform. Suddenly, I feel like I'm in a porn, and I can't help but laugh as I concoct a reason to keep him here longer.

"Can I get you something to drink before you go? We have some bottled water in back."

He grins and his chipped front tooth makes him even sexier. The tousled dark hair and bedroom eyes don't hurt either. Am I seriously thinking of seducing the FedEx guy in my own fucking store? I've clearly lost my mind.

"Thank you, that would be nice."

I get the water for him and he drinks the bottle quickly.

As we stand there, the silence stretches awkwardly as the sexual tension builds. But neither of us makes a move. Normally, this would be my time to come in as Dom and manage the situation, but...I don't. It just doesn't feel right. Instead, I thank him again for waiting and he leaves, a slight frown of disappointment on his lips.

I do a quick check of the shipment, confirming we do indeed have ten boxes of a variety of dildos and sex toys and, in a moment of abandon, I grab a dildo from the top of the box, drop $40 in the cash register and head home.

What? It's product testing.

. . .

When I arrive home, it's late, and I'm ready for bed. I have to get to the store extra early tomorrow to set up the new dildos before we open, and I need a solid eight hours of sleep to function adequately. Always have. I consider it a DNA flaw inherited from my mother.

I've all but forgotten about my new roommate as I turn off my light and lay down, my bed embracing me in luxury. I'm falling into sleep when something knocks against my bedroom wall and someone moans.

And for the next several hours I endure a cacophony of "oh my God" and "you're so huge" and "fuck me harder" and "deeper, oh yes, God!" as Lachlan's bed bangs against my wall. *Great.*

So much for easing in to a having a roommate.

I rummage through my bedside dresser for my earplugs and shove them in my ears, but it doesn't completely block out the sound. I toss and turn all night, with dreams too strange to speak of, and wake with one need. Coffee, with lots of sugar and milk.

In sweats and a robe, I shuffle to the kitchen before my eyes have fully opened. Which is probably for the best. Because there's a nearly naked woman in a g-string standing in front of my open refrigerator. Drinking out of my milk jug.

She smiles when she sees me, her platinum hair artfully styled in the 'just fucked but still sexy' look. "Morning. Hope we didn't keep you up."

I don't even know what to say. I just stand there, looking like one of those cartoon characters with my jaw dropped. She holds out the milk, then frowns into it. "Oops, sorry, I think I drank the last of it. I'm Jessie, by the way. Sorry if we were too loud last night, but God, you know how Lach is." *Jessie*. The one from the store.

I push past her and reach for the coffee pot, until I realize there's no milk and I nearly cry. "Um, no, I don't know what he's like. We're not sleeping together."

"Seriously? Wow. I just assumed. I mean, you two live together. How could you not? He's like a god in bed...I mean, I've been with lots of guys and he's...oh wow. You're missing out."

She shoves the empty milk jug back into the fridge and closes the door, then turns, her perky breasts now staring at me. "If you ever want in, maybe the three of us could..."

"Thank you, but no." Please God, save me from this morning.

As if in answer, Lachlan walks out in jeans and no shirt and for a moment I can see why Jesse assumes all women who glance upon this man's flesh end up fucking him. Because a little part of me...

No. Just stop it, Vi. Not going there.

Lachlan smiles lazily. "Good morning, ladies." His accent is stronger in the morning it seems. "I see you've met. Jessie, why don't you go get dressed and pack up. It's time to go."

She practically skips out of the room. "Sure thing, baby."

I open the fridge, pull out the milk and dump it in the trash, my desperation for coffee and lack of sleep making me unusually angry.

"Sorry about her." He rubs his head and fills a glass of water, downing it in one gulp.

I spin on him and try not to look at his tanned abs of steel, his chiseled chest, his sculpted biceps...but looking at his face doesn't help as much as I'd hoped. He's so *goddamned gorgeous.* "Look, I know you live here and this is your home too, for the time being, so obviously you are free to have houseguests. But please make sure your...*friends*...stay out of my stuff and respect proper social rules, like not walking around my condo naked. Okay?"

He grins, his blue eyes mischievous. "That seems reasonable. It won't happen again."

"Great." I slam the refrigerator closed, unable to find anything that contains enough sugar, caffeine and dairy to assuage me. "I have to get coffee and go to work. Make sure your friend is gone before you leave. And lock up."

I dress quickly and head out without running into either of them again, but as I acquire my morning nectar and start to settle down, I can't help but wonder...just what is it about Lachlan Pierce that makes him a god in bed?

FOUR

Lach

Kill me now. Just do it, before this hangover does.

Or before Vi does. I know she's pissed about Jessie being here. I don't blame her, honestly. I'm not used to worrying about a roommate when I'm fucking.

Jessie is in my room when I go in. She's naked. Not even the g-string left. I think we've made negative progress with the get-her-out-of-the-house plan.

When I sink back into bed, my head still pounding from the rum and my stomach a bit topsy-turvy, she climbs onto my lap, letting her tits hang in my face.

"You want to fuck again?"

I don't know. Let me check with my cock…Nope. Not happening.

She feels my limp dick through the denim and pouts. "Aww, baby. Want me to suck on it?"

I don't say no to blow jobs. It's a core belief of mine.

She kneels before me and pulls off my jeans, taking my none-too-eager cock into her mouth.

It doesn't feel bad…but I'm just…not into it. And it's not because of the booze. I once chugged a whole bottle of vodka and still fucked two girls in an elevator. This is…hmm. Strange.

Jessie pauses her efforts. "Come on, baby. What's wrong?"

I don't know. It's not like Jessie isn't smoking hot. Her tits are worth a grand, literally. And her ass is the result of months at the gym. She isn't too bright, but that's usually a good thing. She'll do anything in bed.

Then why am I not into this?

"Come *on*, baby." She straddles me again, rubbing her wet cunt rubbing against me and nibbling on my neck, whispering in my ear. "I want you to fuck me. Please fuck me, Lachlan."

I try. I really do. But the dick won't stick.

Jessie frowns and pouts some more, but I don't care. She's not girlfriend material, at least not for me. I know she's fooled around with my buddy, Duke. She's probably fucked Darrel, too. I don't judge.

She and I fuck for the same reason. We like it. Simple as that.

"I have to get dressed for work," I say. It's bullshit, but it's not her fault I'm limp. I don't want her to blame herself.

"But baby, I want to feel you." This is what I like about Jessie. Well, what I *liked*. I could always count on her for a good fuck. But now…suddenly now that doesn't seem enough.

Strange.

"I have to go."

She bites her lip, considering. "You can fuck me without a condom."

Fuck no. I use condoms. It's another core belief.

I slide her off my lap, zip up my jeans, and throw on a Michael Jackson t-shirt. "It's time for you to go."

"Fine." She pulls on her dress. It doesn't cover much. "I'll see if Duke has time."

"Go ahead." I don't care. I don't get jealous.

She walks out, slamming the door shut behind her, and I collapse on the bed. I'm going to need to make things up to Vi. I try to think of a peace offering, but fuck it, my head hurts too much, so I just think of Vi. Her full lips, her thighs. The curve of her ass. And now my cock comes to life.

An unfamiliar feeling enters me. I can't quite name it. Whatever it is, I know one thing.

I really hope Vi is single.

FIVE

Vi

Zoe is still giggling about Lachlan as we close up the store. "Think he'll still shop here?" she asks, her big anime eyes glistening from mirthful tears.

"I have no idea," I say, unable to suppress my own laughter, because the whole thing is just ludicrous. "Hopefully he does. I think he's single-handedly kept our little venture afloat the last few months."

While not specifically true, he's definitely contributed to the profit margin.

We reach our cars and hug. Her smile fades as she gets in and I know why. "Henry still?"

She nods and now those tears in her eyes aren't from laughter. "He wants to marry me so we're not living in sin, but I want to wait until we've resolved our issues."

"Marriage won't make things better."

She starts her engine and sighs. "I know. That's what I told him."

"What did he say?"

"That I'm too much of a temptation and he has to put his faith first. I told him if he really feels that way then maybe we shouldn't live together. But he doesn't want to move out, either. And since we live in my house, that I own, I'm not leaving. We're at an impasse."

Asshole. "You could always kick him out."

She shrugs and gets into her car. "I'm not there yet."

I frown, and she flashes a small rueful smile as she pulls out of the spot next to mine. Waving, I climb into my cherry apple red '97 Camaro. My car purrs to life and I sigh happily as I press the gas.

Leaving behind my worry for Zoe, my mood shifts as I drive out of town to my best friend Kacie's house. There's much squealing, hugging, and pecking of cheeks as I lug a bag of gifts into her spacious and beautiful home.

"You look so good," I tell her as we hug one more time. "I feel like it's been forever since we've seen each other."

She tosses a lock of blond hair off her shoulder and smiles, her blue eyes so happy. "I know. Babies and work. That's my life in a nutshell." But she's grinning madly when she says it, and I know she loves every minute.

"I hope there's time for Dr. Sexy in there somewhere?"

As if on cue, the man walks into the living room. "Oh, I make sure of it," Sebastian says as he kisses his wife's head. She grins and wraps an arm around him.

"You two are to-die-for cute, you know that?"

They both nod as Sebastian kisses her one more time, this time full on the lips. "Work called. I've got to check on a patient, but I'll be back in a few hours. I trust you ladies will survive without me?"

Kacie laughs. "We'll manage somehow. But hurry home. I have plans for you later."

I mock groan and leave them in a liplock as I go in search of my godbabies. I find them upstairs in their nursery, just waking from a nap. Adele and Daniel. The two cutest twins in the entire planet both smile up at me from their shared crib—they refused to sleep apart—and I reach for them both, dropping a kiss on each fuzzy head before picking up Adele to change her diaper. Switch, repeat, and it's go time.

With one baby in each arm I make my way down the stairs. "I have presents for you both!" I tell them, smiling. "Do you want to open presents?" The babies coo excitedly at my tone.

Once Sebastian leaves and the babies settle into our laps enjoying the discovery of their fingers more than any gifts I could bring, Kacie and I juggle cups of coffee and catch each other up on everything we've missed in the last few weeks.

"Hitched is taking off faster than we can keep up," she says. She and her twin brother, Tate, run a premiere bachelor and bachelorette party planning company here in Las Vegas, which got major exposure when they snagged a party for a prominent magician in town and he told all of his celebrity friends. This was right before Kacie and Dr. Sexy, the prominent pediatric surgeon Sebastian Donovan, got engaged after a crazy summer following a drunken night that led to marriage.

You know, because Vegas.

"I'm thrilled for you! And the babies are getting so big. I have to come over more or I'll show up one day and they'll be in college." We switch babies so I can hold Adele for a while.

"Stop it. Don't give them ideas. I swear they conspire with each other behind my back on how to take over the world."

I laugh. "I'm sure your mother felt the same way about you and Tate."

"Ha! That's probably true. And look at us now. Guess she was right." She sips her decaf coffee and my heart goes out to her. Nursing is a sacrifice. "Now, enough about me. Tell me about you! How's Whipped, how's life, how's Zoe, how's everything? Details, woman!"

I tell her all, saving the best for last. Lachlan.

Her mouth forms an O as I talk about last night.

"Can you believe his fucking kept me up all night?"

I expect her to be outraged on my behalf, as is the job of the best friend in these situations. But instead she grins in the way I know means trouble and raises an eyebrow. "All night? With wall-banging enthusiasm? So, let me get this straight. He's got a sexy accent, he's hot as hell, washboard abs, the face of a god, all night stamina and he can go hard long enough to shake the walls? And he's willing to give you no-strings attached pleasure? Um, why aren't you hitting that?"

"Why? Did you not hear anything I said?"

She wags her eyebrows suggestively. "Oh, I did. And that's the point. Is he serious about the girl from this morning?"

"No, I don't think he knows what serious means. I'd probably have to buy him a dictionary for him to understand that word."

"Then you need to discover this man's skills for yourself." She sets her coffee mug down and reaches for my hand. "I say this with all the love of a best friend: Vi, you need to get fucked hard and good and by a man who knows how. It's been too long."

I laugh at the deadly serious expression on her face but shake my head. "Nope, not happening. Not with him."

"And not with the sexy FedEx man," she says.

"Because I'm not starring in a porn!"

"And not with anyone else, either. You said he's only living there for a few months. So what could it hurt?"

"It could make these next few months impossible."

She cocks her head and pulls out a breast to nurse Daniel. "Fine, if not with him, then with someone. Just go out and have fun. I'd drag you out myself but, well, it'll be awhile before I spend a night on the town drinking."

We spend a few more hours talking, laughing and playing with babies until Sebastian comes home and I can tell I'll soon be the third wheel. We put the babies to bed and I leave with more hugs for them both.

On the way home that night I consider my friend's advice and decide, you know what? Fuck it. She's right. I need to get laid. I head to Spanked, a fetish sex club I used to frequent to find new clients and scratch my own personal itches from time to time. I could always count on it for finding a willing sub who was ready to play. I park and walk to the door. The bouncer, Brent, recognizes me and waves. "Vi, it's been too long. Welcome back."

"Thanks, Brent. How's it going in there tonight?"

Brent, a sub with model-like good looks who often passed clients to me, shrugs his well-defined shoulders. "A bit slow, but I think you'll find what you need. You taking any new clients, or still just focused on Whipped?"

"Just the shop. I'll let you know if that changes."

He opens the door and lets me in. "I got some clients for you if it does change. You're the best out there and everyone knows it."

I kiss his cheek as I walk in. "Thanks, Brent. You're sweet."

"Anything for you, Vi. Have fun tonight."

I intend to.

The club is dark, with beams of colored light projecting through the room like lasers. On the dance floor couples sway to loud music that feels like it's inside of me, beating out its own rhythm in my blood. One couple is mostly naked, already engaged in more than just dance, but no one seems to mind.

There's an all-you-can-eat open buffet to the right of the dance floor and several people in various states of undress are pilling up their plates. Fucking and dancing takes carbs and stamina, but no way have I ever eaten here. I shudder just imagining what has made its way into that food.

While downstairs may offer newbies a peep or two, upstairs is where all the action is. As I head up, a woman dressed in a leather corset and not much else guides a man on all fours with a leash. He's muzzled and wearing a loincloth. I recognize the woman as another Dom and nod a greeting to her as we pass on the staircase.

Upstairs, you can smell the sex. It's everywhere. In one corner, a raised bed is set up off the floor, with stirrups for feet. On it, a naked, writhing woman is strapped down while one man eats her pussy and another two suck at her tits. The erotic naughtiness of it makes me wet, and I watch as the man eating her stands, slips a condom on his extra-large cock, and shoves it into her. She cries out and one of the men still sucking on her tits lets his hand fall to her clit. He rubs it while the other guy fucks her and for a moment I wish I was in her place. Just for a moment.

One of the guys nods to me when he sees me watching. He lets go of the nipple long enough to smile and ask me if I want to be next.

I hesitate. Do I? It could fix my problem fast. When I imagine myself strapped down I shudder and shake my head. "Thank you, but no. Have fun."

He grins and goes back to the breast while I walk past them and into the den of anything goes. It's a room reserved for hard core BDSM. Normally it's even too heavy for me, but tonight I'm curious. I peek in and watch as all manner of kink is acted out by willing partners. A woman whipping her sub. Another man licking her heels.

It does nothing for me.

The ache is still there. I want something. But not this. And not those guys fucking that girl. And certainly not my sexy new roommate. But *something*.

I half-consider calling Chad, but it's a thought that ends before it's fully formed. He deserves more than a booty call and I can't give him more.

If I hook up with anyone here, I know how the night will play out. A little kink, a good fuck and I'll go home alone. I could get myself off without all this effort.

I've had too much of this, and realize I'm no longer in the mood. It's why I haven't been here in a while. Why I was ready to give up my work as a Dom, even though I never got sexual with clients. Why I knew it was time for a change. For Whipped. For…something *more* in my personal life.

I could have had that something more with Chad. He was the perfect sub and a great guy. Gorgeous, talented, my friends liked him. We even played house for a brief moment. But… it wasn't right.

Now, I don't even know what I'm looking for.

I ditch my plans for a night of nothing and head home, ready to strip off the tight clothes and leather accessories and just relax.

But I'm surprised to find Lachlan home. For some reason, I expected him to be out partying or something. I'm even more surprised when he holds out a bag with a bow on it when I walk in the door.

"My white flag," he says by way of explanation.

I accept it and pull out the contents. It's a new jug of milk. I smile at him, genuinely grateful for this kindness. It means coffee in the morning. "Thank you. I appreciate this."

I stick it in the fridge and lean against the counter, looking more closely at him. His eyes are still a bit bloodshot and he's rubbing the back of his neck. Last night must have been rough on him. "Still hungover, huh?"

He cocks his head. "Yeah. I got a bit fucked up. Something about a bottle or two of rum…it's a bit murky after that."

I laugh as I move through the kitchen collecting ingredients for my famous hangover cure. "I bet. Rum is a sneaky bitch, no doubt."

"That she is." He eyes my assortment of foods suspiciously. "What are you making?"

"Your savior. Avert your eyes, this is a closely held family recipe that none but our kin are privy to."

He turns away as I add things to the blender and hit the button, causing him to flinch from the noise. When I'm done, I hand him a glass filled to the brim with a thick greenish brown sludge. "Drink it all. Every last drop. You'll thank me after."

"If I'm not dead," he says, his accent lingering over the words.

He chugs it all, and I give him props for keeping it down. Not everyone does. I count to ten in my mind and see the moment it starts affecting him.

His grin widens, spreading to his eyes. "That's amazing. You're a witch. A beautiful, brilliant, mad witch. I think I might be in love."

"Settle down, cowboy, it's just a drink, not a proposal. But I'm glad it helped."

"Me, too. I'm working tonight, and you just saved my ass."

Of course I have to look at said ass as he walks into the living room, and I pat myself on the back for saving something so very perfect.

"What do you do?" I ask to keep my mind off his body parts.

He grins that infuriating tease of a grin. "You should come and see. 10pm. Bring your friends. Do you still have the cards I gave you?"

I hang my head in shame. "No."

He laughs and hands me a few more.

The cards are thick, quality and my curiosity is definitely piqued. "Are you like a musician or something?"

"If you're wondering if I'm good with my hands..."

"No. I'm not wondering." Not even a little. But his hands are big.

God.

He winks at me, grabs his keys and kisses my cheek. "Thanks for the hangover cure. I owe you. Have a great night. I won't be back 'til morning."

He leaves me standing there, his kiss still burning my cheek and sending warmth through my body as I consider what I will do the rest of the evening.

I wander to the kitchen table and piece together a few bits of the puzzle. There are times I can get lost in this, in the intricate shapes and the way only certain pieces fit together. You can't force a piece to fit. Some come close, and might look good initially, but if it isn't a perfect match the bigger picture will be ruined.

Tonight, however, the puzzle isn't holding my attention.

I consider cleaning the apartment. It's already a mess again. I pick up a few dishes and put them in the sink, but that's as far as I get. Cleaning isn't really my favorite thing in the world.

I could read, but I'm in between books and don't have the energy to dive into something new.

Damn Lachlan. He's distracting me, and I don't like being distracted.

In a moment of inspiration, I remember my impromptu purchase of that new dildo that's still in my purse, and I reach for it, pull it out of the packaging and stare at it. It vibrates, has a clit stimulator and is purple. It should do the job just fine.

I kick off my boots, unzip my leather skirt and slip out of it, pull off my blouse and sink into the shabby chic living room chair, spreading my legs as I imagine...

Lachlan.

Fuck.

Whatever. This is my private fantasy, privy to no one else. I let myself have it. The fantasy of those long fingers, those soft lips, and all the other parts I imagine are quite effective. I'm wet and swollen, ready to be filled as I slip the dildo inside of me. The vibration rubs against my clit, and I squeeze a nipple as I surrender to the fantasy that Lachlan is inside of me. His hands on my tits. His lips on my neck. I climax, moaning and—

The door to the condo swings open. Lachlan stands there, his eyes wide, a bulge appearing quite suddenly in his pants. "Holy fuck!" he says, still staring.

Oh my fucking God. "Get out! What the fuck! Get out! Close your eyes!" I'm scrambling to find something to cover me, but there's nothing but a throw pillow.

It takes him a moment but he closes his eyes finally.

"Now get out."

"I can't fucking see," he says, still standing there.

"Too bad. What are you even *doing* here? I thought you wouldn't be back until morning!"

"I forgot some of my bag," he says. He stumbles around the room and manages to grab his backpack by the door. Before I can get my clothes back on he turns around, his eyes open now. "You know, if you ever want the real thing—"

Mother*fucker*. I throw my dildo at him and he catches it in one hand and glances at it. "Huh. You might want to go bigger next time." Smirking, he drops the purple cock on the counter and walks out.

SIX

Lach

I'm in a meeting with an elderly woman who might invest in my youth center. We're sitting at her high-end kitchen table in her old money mansion. And I'm as hard as a fucking rock.

I blame Vi.

Miss Wallace and I were discussing renovating the Spacey Mall, when she suggested red for the furniture. Then I thought of Vi's hair.

Then I thought of her legs spread on the arm chair and... Anyway, I need to think of something else. I have an iron rod for a cock now, and it needs to go. When we conclude the meeting, Miss Wallace will want to shake my hand. Maybe even hug. You see the problem.

And if you don't, if you're thinking it can't possibly be that big, then I feel sorry for you. Men like me are out there. Trust me.

"Is everything okay, Mr. Pierce?"

I shuffle in my chair, trying to keep my knees from hitting the table and knocking my delicate tea cup over, saucer and all. "Yes. I was just thinking red is the perfect color."

A young Hispanic woman comes in from the kitchen and pours us more coffee. When her eyes catch my lap, she blushes and walks quickly out of the room.

Great.

Miss Wallace doesn't notice. She gives me a big smile. "So in conclusion…"

Fuck. I'm running out of time. I call to mind everything I know about losing an erection, tricks I learned in middle school.

Math.

$2 + 2 = Vi.$

Fuck.

Distraction. Nature. Trees.

A stick.

Vi and a dildo.

Fuck.

Imagining my best friend's grandmother.

Fuck no.

I discreetly pull out my phone, keeping it in my lap, and Google "how to get rid of boner."

Miss Wallace leans forward over her paperwork. "An important text message?"

I grin. "An emergency." The Google search provides an answer. Squeeze your thighs, and the blood will leave your erection. I give it a go. Huh. It actually works.

I stuff the phone back in my pocket. "It's handled."

"Great." She closes her folder. "Well, I think we're about done."

"So you're interested?"

"Very." She smiles. I smile back. With her support, I won't have to go on tour.

We stand. She goes in for a hug. There is no steel pole between us. The crisis is averted.

Fucking Vi. As I leave the immaculate house through the high double doors, I imagine Vi spread out on the couch again, naked except for a pair of high heels, her finger on her clit. Oh, she wasn't wearing high heels, you say?

Well, fuck you, it's my fantasy.

SEVEN

Vi

I can't stand it. Despite being caught masturbating by Lachlan, I still have this overwhelming urge to show up at his work and find out what he does for a living.

I'm not one to easily embarrass. Even what happened today didn't really embarrass me as much as it...oh God, turned me on.

There, I said it. Happy?

So my hesitation in showing up at his work tonight isn't from shame. After all, I was doing nothing wrong. I just don't want to give him, or myself, the wrong idea. Because I am not getting involved with the sexy Australian, no matter how big his cock might or might not be.

But in the end, I relent, and call up my friends. Zoe says yes immediately. Kacie takes very little convincing, despite her earlier protest that she won't be hitting the town anytime soon. "Sebastian is already nodding his encouragement. He's got the babies and enough pumped milk to get through the night. I'll call Tate and have him play chauffeur to pick everyone up. Just say when."

When is now. And we are parking at the Wynn, still unsure about what we're about to see.

"He gave you no hints as to his show?" Tate asks. As the only guy in our little group when Sebastian's not with us, Tate likes to walk as if we are his arm candy. Something none of us actually put up with. But he certainly doesn't mind being surrounded by three beautiful women, even if one of those women is his twin.

Zoe nudges Tate and smiles. "We're taking bets about what he does. Want in?"

"What are my choices?" Tate asks, looking down at our petite friend.

If I'd had any worries Zoe would fit in with my friends when we first decided to go into business together—which I really didn't—they were quickly assuaged when I saw her with everyone. She fits right in, even if she has to look up to make eye contact with anyone.

"We've got magician, acrobat, singer, musician," she says, listing them one by one.

"Which did Vi pick?" he asks, winking at me with his dark eyes.

"She didn't. She said she refuses to wager on him."

I laugh at her impersonation of me. "Oh stop it, you guys. We're here."

I hand the gold cards to the concierge. "Lachlan Pierce said to give his name."

The middle-aged man behind the table nods. "Of course, please follow me. You ladies are in for a real treat tonight."

He glances at Tate and his mouth twitches. "And you too, sir."

We're taken into an auditorium and given seats front row center of the stage. As the rest of the seats fill, Tate looks around, a panicked expression on his handsome face. "Ladies...I think we might have been very wrong about Mr. Pierce's career."

"What's wrong?" I ask, and I realize what's bothering him. He might be the only man in the audience. It's full of women.

The lights go down and the crowd, instead of quieting, as is typical for a show, erupts into wild cheers.

Music fills the room and colored lights flicker over the black stage as a man does a double flip onto the stage.

I grab Kacie's hand. "Holy shit!"

"What?"

"That's Lachlan!"

He's joined by several other men who begin to do astonishing acrobatics across the stage before they start to dance.

"I can't fucking believe this!" Tate says. And the three of us are nearly in tears from laughing as Tate glares at us. "You took me to a fucking male strip show!"

I want to rib him more but Lachlan is taking center stage for an impressive solo that shows he's a lot more than just a pretty face and a hard body. He's seriously fucking talented. Like, massively so. I can't help but be impressed as he does things with his body I can't imagine being able to do.

Tate is still moaning something next to me about how this can never be forgiven and how I'll owe him eternally for this, but my eyes are locked on the beautiful man on stage.

Kacie leans into me. "This is the man you won't sleep with?"

I nod wordlessly, and she just shakes her head.

I'm beginning to agree with her assessment of my sanity as I watch what he does with his hips.

All those feelings change when the tone of the music shifts and Lachlan steps off the stage and comes right toward me. Someone announces that they need an audience member volunteer for the next dance.

Every woman in the audience—which I'm beginning to think is every woman in Las Vegas by the sound—is clamoring to be chosen.

Except me.

But Lachlan ignores my reluctance and pulls me on stage with him at my friends' encouragement. He sits me down on a chair as a spotlight blinds me to everyone but him.

Smoke fills the stage and the music turns slower, more erotic.

He begins to dance over me, pulling my hands around his hard body until they are on his ass. God, this man's ass is a study in perfection.

As he moves my hands over his body, he gyrates over me, grinding himself between my legs as his mouth hovers over my neck. With a flash of movement, he pulls his pants off and I stare, dumbstruck, at his mostly naked body, a bit of silver cloth all that remains between his cock and the rest of the world, and it's looking pretty stretched out as he grows.

He leans in again, and I feel his hard-on press against me.

"See anything you like?" he asks.

"There was a delicious looking steak on the menu at the restaurant we went to."

He shakes his head, still smiling. "I worry about your priorities."

"Oh, sex is high up there. Just not with you."

He falls back as if wounded, then keeps dancing close to me. "I understand. You're like a virgin." I nearly choke at that, but he keeps talking. "You just don't know what you're missing. Yet."

That 'yet' hovers in the air as I'm escorted back to my seat to watch the rest of the show.

After the show we are all still stuck to our seats as the rest of the women in the audience swarm the stage.

"Oh, Vi, this is horrible," Tate says. "Whenever I think of you now, I see things. Terrible things."

Kacie laughs. "I think you owe him therapy."

"They're not even fully naked," I argue.

Tate just shakes his head. "My mind fills in the blanks."

So does mine. God, so does mine. Especially since I can still feel the way his cock pressed between my legs. Hard. Throbbing. Ready.

I'm ready to get out of there, to get some air and some clarity and, most importantly, some distance. Instead, one of the dancers blocks our escape and escorts us back stage. "Lachlan said you're friends of his and deserve the VIP treatment. Follow me."

I try to resist but Kacie and Zoe are having none of it, and even Tate seems intent on torturing me. "It's payback, my dear," he whispers into my ear. "You must face this man."

I'm breathless by the time Lachlan finds us. My friends have all been wooed away by tables of food, glasses of champagne and scantily clad sexy men.

I get pulled into Lachlan's dressing room, which he locks behind him.

He's still wearing just the…I don't know, loincloth? His body glistens with oil and sweat and makes his muscles ripple under the light. His blond hair is a wild halo of lust around his perfect face, framing every desire I have for him.

Every desire I want to resist.

"We have to talk," I say.

He grabs me and pulls me to him, our bodies pressed against each other. "Not with words," he says against my ear lobe. "Body language is better."

And I can't deny him. Part of me wants to. And though I'd like to blame it on the champagne that is already fuzzing my brain, I know this craving for him predated the alcohol.

So when he pulls up my skirt and runs his hands over my body with barely contained urgency, I don't resist.

And when he pushes me against the wall and spreads my legs with his hard thighs, I don't pull away. No, instead I lean into him and eagerly take in everything he gives me, moaning as his finger pulls aside my underwear and teases my clit.

"I need you, Vi," he says as he pushes his finger into me while rubbing the swollen nub.

It is more than I imagined. More than my dildo could ever hope to replicate. More than my mind could conceive. The scent of his body so close, the feel of his hard muscles holding me. His finger inside of me, filling me with one, then two, finding every spot of pleasure.

I don't think. Don't analyze the pros and cons. I don't let myself consider that I'm not in control. That this shouldn't be happening. I give into the sensation of leaving behind everything but the here and now of this man pressed against me.

His mouth is on mine, our tongues teasing each other. He tastes like mint. Like madness and magic and I imagine that tongue on other places on my body.

It doesn't take long for my orgasm to build, and just before it breaks inside of me, he pulls out his finger. I moan, disappointed, empty, and he smiles, slides a condom onto his cock and lifts me off the ground, his hands under my ass, holding me against his body. He presses me against the wall and I wrap my legs around him as he shoves his cock deep into me.

He's huge. Thick and long and I worry he'll tear me, but with a few more pumps he's stretched me into taking him all the way and as his fingers dig into my ass and my nails dig into his back, he fucks me harder than I've ever been fucked before.

I bite his neck and hear him groan and fuck harder.

He dominates me and as I come on his cock and he explodes inside me, I realize how much I love it and want it and need it.

Someone knocks on the dressing room door, breaking the magic between us and reminding me where I am and who I'm with. I pull out of Lach's arms as he releases my legs, but standing proves a bit precarious as I'm still wobbly from two orgasms in the space of ten minutes.

Lachlan hands me my panties. "Next time you'll get the all-night treatment."

Next time?

Oh, *hell* no.

But I don't have time to respond because someone is shouting through the door. "Yo, Lach, time to party. Get your ass out here."

I squeeze past him, pulling myself together, and fling open the door to face one of the dancers in his group.

Lachlan comes up behind me and places his hand on my lower back. "Vi, this is Duke. Duke, Vi."

Duke raises an eyebrow. "I see why you didn't want to hang with us. I wouldn't either."

I push past him, leaving the warmth of Lach's hand. "Nice to meet you."

I don't stay to chat, instead I make my way through the hall until I find my friends. "It's time to go," I tell them. Tate is about to argue but Kacie takes a good look at me, gives him the twin stare and they nod in unison. Zoe's flirting with one of the dancers but pulls herself away when Tate taps her shoulder.

Not a lot of talking happens in the car. Instead, I sit in the front and blast the radio, drowning out any words that might pull the story of what happened from me. I'm just not ready to talk about it. Honestly, I'm still lost in that moment and unsure how I feel.

We drop Kacie off first. Her breasts are about to burst with milk, she informs us, making Tate gag dramatically. Brothers. Then Zoe, who once again looks depressed to be going home. *Seriously, girl, dump that asshole,* I mentally plead with her.

And then I'm alone with Tate, who turns off the music and forbids me from turning it back on.

"Spill, Vi. What happened?"

"I fucked Lachlan," I say without preamble. Tate laughs, and I punch him in the shoulder. "This is so not funny."

"It kinda is. This isn't a crisis. This is a good thing. If I were gay I'd have done him after that dance," he says.

"Yeah, well, you're not living with him, are you? I have to face him every day now, and I don't know what to say to him." I turn to look at my other best friend. He's gorgeous and knows it. Opposite in looks to Kacie, ironically, with dark hair but those same piercing blue eyes as his sister. "You're a womanizer who sleeps with anyone with tits, maybe you can help me with this."

"Well, when you put it so nicely..."

"You know what I mean. Lach is a player. I need to know what he'd be expecting right now."

Tate shrugs. "Vi, I'm always honest with the women I'm with, and from what you've said, it sounds like he is too. So just be honest. Tell him what you want. If this was a one-time thing for you, then tell him you don't want anything more with him."

He glances over at me as I fidget with a seat-belt that was just fine left alone, and raises an eyebrow.

"Unless you *do* want more?"

EIGHT

Lach

I'm a male stripper.

I'm not ashamed of it. I turn girls on five nights a week. With a stare. With a sway of the hips. Then I take them home and fuck their brains out. If I ever see them again, it's only for sex.

At least it used to be. Tonight was different.

Tonight I wanted more.

After Vi left, I collapsed in my makeup chair. Now, as my buddies change and prepare for a night of partying, I plan my next move. Nothing comes to mind. I come to a conclusion.

I'm fucked.

I broke the roommate agreement.

Vi isn't interested in a fuckbuddy. I've never been any-thing else. High school was a series of one-night stands. And stripping, well…Women love hooking up with a stripper. Dating said stripper as he seduces different women each night, not so much. My buddy Ricky made the monogamous stripper thing work. It's possible with the right girl. But that's not Vi. And honestly, that's not me.

My contract's over in a few months.

Because as much as I love dancing and making women drool—and trust me, it's a lot—I love helping people more. I know what it's like to need a hand. My parents didn't help. Dad spent his nights meeting his high school buddies at bars and hooking up with college girls. Mom spent her nights cuddled up with a bottle of gin and watching reruns of her favorite 'stories.' She said Dad was stuck in the glory days. He said Mom was an ugly old bitch. They both called me a dumbass. Which I was. I almost ended up in juvie. But I didn't.

Because of Darrel. He caught me selling weed. I was trying to make an extra buck. He showed me a better way. He taught me how to dance. He kept an eye on me. He didn't set me on the best path. But it was a better one. Did he become a dick later? Yes. Was he using me from the start? Maybe.

But I'll always be grateful for his help. With it, I made a lot of money. And now, I'm ready to give back.

So I'm opening a youth center. Name pending. I'm making it the best I can. If I have to tour again for the money, I might. But I don't want to.

I want to spend my days teaching kids, and my nights cuddling with Vi.

Much to my own amazement, I'm ready to be boyfriend material.

Now how the fuck do I go about it?

"Hey, Ricky. How'd you and Martha meet?"

He flips on a sleeveless jacket and strokes his blond goatee. He's the oldest member of the Aussie Posse. Another couple of years, and he'll be too old. He plans to sell custom furniture. I'm glad the guy has a wife. Some days, I think he's got it better than any of us.

"We met at a woodworking class." He polishes his glasses. He doesn't wear them during the show. "It took me a week to ask her out. I gave her a necklace I made. She said 'why not?'"

Duke leaves his chair, slaps Ricky on the shoulder. "Still don't know why you did that, buddy." His black beard runs up the side of his face, wolverine style. He's a huge guy. Bigger than me. He has the second largest number of solos. When my contract is over, he'll take my place.

Ricky chuckles. "All I know is, every night I fall asleep with the woman of my dreams."

Duke grins. "I fall asleep with two."

Ricky nods, smiling. He's used to this kind of taunting. The guys don't get why he'd settle down when there's a fresh pussy to fuck each night. I'm starting to side more with Ricky now, though.

"Don't worry, Ricky," I say. "Duke gets two girls a night, but they all leave him the next day. Wonder why?"

"I don't do emotional crap," says Duke. "And next day, things get soft real fast."

I rub my chin thoughtfully. "Huh. That's what she said."

The guys laugh. Duke frowns. Sorry, Dukey. But I don't stand for taunting couples. Not since I decided to be part of one. Even if it's only been a few hours.

"You have a problem with me?" asks Duke. He walks up to me. I'm still sitting. Fuck, the guy is huge.

I give him my most charming smile. "No problem."

Duke snickers. "Then don't be a fucking hypocrite. I saw you tapping that redhead tonight. What a fucking slut. You get her number? I could use a good ass—"

I jump up and my fist slams into his jaw. He stumbles back. "Don't fucking talk about her," I growl.

He rubs blood off his lip. He smiles. "You little cock-sucker." He slams into me. It's like being slammed by a wall. My back smashes against a mirror. It shatters.

There's a code of conduct when two men fight. I don't give a fuck. I knee him in the balls.

Duke collapses on the floor. I expect him to clasp his precious jewels in pain. Instead, he grabs my leg and yanks me down. I fall on broken glass. It crunches. He climbs on top of me. He raises a fist.

"What's happening here?" The voice is deep and loud. It's Darrel. He stands at the doorway to the dressing room. He wears a white suit.

Duke crawls off me. "Lach lost his fucking mind."

I want to say some witty comeback, but the adrenaline is wearing off, and my back is on fire.

Darrel walks through the room and towers over me. "Since when do we attack our fellow brothers?"

I speak through a clenched jaw. "He's not my fucking brother."

Darrel shakes his head. "What's happening to you, Lach?" He crouches down and wipes something off my forehead. I smack his hand away. He frowns. "You think you're better than us?"

I don't answer.

He yells. "You think you don't need us anymore?"

I don't acknowledge him. I stand up and grab my jacket. Glass still digs into my skin. I'll deal with it later. "I'll see you tomorrow."

"Take tomorrow off."

I turn back to him. "What?"

"You're off tomorrow. Use the day to get your shit together. Until you do, Duke has your solos."

"Fine with me." I'm done soon anyway.

Darrel smiles. "Fine. As long as you're not soloing, your pay is cut in half."

I curl my fist. It's covered in blood. "You can't fucking do that. We have a contract."

"And you're not living up to your end."

Fuck this. I don't need the extra money that bad. My investor will come through. As I leave, Darrel pats Duke on the shoulder and congratulates the guys on a great show. They smile and nod. They act like children around him. I remember when I did the same.

. . .

I drop by a clinic on my way home. They remove the glass from my back. The pieces are small. I don't even need stitches. The whole time, I think of Vi. I need to talk to her, tell her what I want. Ricky kicked things off with a gift, so I head to a store and pick out something appropriate.

When I enter the apartment, Vi jumps off the couch. She's wearing a blue sweater. Her face is red. An open bottle of white wine is on her desk.

I want to throw her back on the couch and tear her clothes off. But I resist. I close the door behind me. "I need to tell you something."

"Me first." She waves her hands as she talks. Her words slur. "I know you don't do relationships. I knew it when we had sex. So, I'm not expecting anything. But I'm not interested in a fuckbuddy. I know that's what you want, and that's okay. No judgment. One of my best friends is the same. But right now, I need someone steady. Someone I can rely on."

I grin. "That's nice. Now, will you go out with me?"

Her mouth drops open. "…What?"

I pull the gift out of my bag and hand it to her. "Will you go out with me?"

NINE

Vi

I'm spent. I spoke literally all the words and expected him to be relieved, to agree, to at most argue for more stringless sex. Not to ask me out on a real date. And give me a gift?

I open my mouth to say no, to explain what a bad idea this is.

"Yes," I say, then cover my betraying bastard of a mouth with my hand. "Wait, no—"

Lachlan's smile is reminiscent of the cat that ate the canary. "No, too late."

I drop my hand and cross my arms over my chest. "I can change my mind if I want…"

He raises an eyebrow. "And show yourself to be inconsistent with your word?"

"I'm not inconsistent. But what's the point of going out together?" It's getting hot in this condo, and I start pacing the small living room, wrapped gift still in hand. Bigger than a breadbox. Sort of. Longer than a breadbox?

Lachlan seems too laid back and relaxed, and it pisses me off just a little. "I believe the point is to see if two people are compatible in a long-term relationship," he explains, as if talking to a child.

That stops me in my pacing. I look up at him. "And you're interested in that? A long-term relationship?"

He shrugs. "I don't know. Maybe. With the right person."

My heart flutters, and I mentally smack it down. Not now, silly heart. I've gotta use my head for this one. "And you think I'm the right person?"

He reaches for my hand, brushing a thumb over my skin and making me shiver. His blue eyes are so bright as he stares into mine. "I think you could be. If we got to know each other better, we'd find out. That's the point of dating." He winks at me and pulls me closer to him, our bodies now just a sliver apart. So close I can feel his heart beat. "You should open your gift."

I almost forgot I have a gift. He pulls away enough for me to peel open the red wrapping paper. Inside is a new puzzle, one I've had my eye on for a while. "How did you know I wanted this?"

He shrugs and smiles. "Lucky guess? I thought we could work on it together."

I'm stunned. This is quite possibly one of the sweetest things a guy has ever done for me. I set the puzzle down on the chair next to me. "Thank you."

He comes close again, brushing a strand of hair off my cheek with the pad of his thumb. "I know it's sudden. But I think we could make this work, Vi. You and me. And," he says, a mischievous glint coming into his eye, "we have the advantage of knowing we're sexually compatible."

I pull back, walking backwards, my heart slamming into my gut. Because this is the problem. He just doesn't know it yet. I feel my mouth blurt out my thoughts. "That's where you're wrong. That's what you don't understand—but, of course how could you? We are the opposite of compatible. Unless you're secretly a submissive—in which case you do a really great impersonation of a Dom."

He frowns. "What the fuck are you talking about, Vi?"

I rush ahead. "Subs? Doms? The lifestyle? Which you are clearly not a part of. I was a professional Dom for the last five years before opening my store. It wasn't just work for me, it's also my preferred kink sexually. My *strong* preference. This—" I wave my hands between us, "this…this *thing*—it won't work."

He strides over to me again, his long legs spanning the living room in just a few steps until he has me backed against the wall, his arms encircling my waist. "I don't know about that stuff." His cock presses into my belly as his hand presses into my lower back, and his head bends so that his lips brush against my cheek. "All I know, Vi, is that it *did* work. You came twice in my dressing room. And that wasn't even my best work."

I want to resist him, to pull away, but I'm lost in his gaze, trapped by the magnetic pull of his arms around me. My heart beats hard and fast in my chest. And I'm shocked to realize I want to surrender to this man, to have him make me his, to feel him take me, hard and fast and deep.

His hands drop to my ass as he pulls our hips closer. His lips trace a line of fire over my neck and to my lips. "Isn't it possible that what you think you know about yourself is just a small piece of a much bigger puzzle? Maybe this is an opportunity to discover more of who you really are."

Before I can answer him, his lips are on mine, his tongue teasing as our kiss deepens, and I lose myself in the passion of our embrace. Every part of my body is on fire for him. He could take me here, now, against the wall, through our clothes, and I wouldn't care. I would open for him because I need him inside me. Now.

But he pulls away and takes all that heat with him, and I feel my body wilt just a little. His grin is maddening as he straightens the pants that are so very clearly bulging. "I'm sorry, but I don't have sex until at least the third date." He leaves for his own bedroom.

And I resist the urge to throw a pillow at his head.

I can't breathe I'm so turned on. And before he closes his bedroom door, he says, "I believe the toy you're looking for is in the top drawer."

I open the drawer and grab my new dildo as I stomp to my own bedroom.

TEN

Lach

Vi bounces on my cock, clenching it with her tight pussy. Actually, she's in the other room, masturbating. I'm on my bed, fantasizing. The walls are thin, and I hear her moan as she builds up to climax. I unzip my jeans and start rubbing my cock. This three dates thing is harder than I thought, and it's only been ten minutes. All I want is Vi. Her tits. Her ass. Her pussy. I imagine sucking on her nipples as she rides me. Pressing her lips against mine as we move together. I want her to come. I hear her gasp in the other room. She climaxes. I come.

Fuck. Why did I propose this date thing again?

The next morning, I wake to the sound of my phone ringing and a serious case of wood from a night of dreams filled with Vi.

I answer the phone begrudgingly, wishing I were still in that dream.

It's Mrs. Wallace. "I looked over your proposal, Mr. Pierce. I love your plans for the center, but I think we'll have to raise prices."

And just like that, the wood is gone. "Raise prices?"

"We'll barely break even with the current plan. But don't worry. I see potential for real profit."

I grab the glass of water by my bed and take a sip. My hands tremble. "Profit isn't the point. The center needs to help people. Not put them in debt."

Mrs. Wallace laughs. Like one laughs at a little child who thinks they're clever. "I'm sorry. But we're not catering to the homeless here."

"I intend to help those who need help."

"Not with my money, you're not."

Fuck. I can't have this deal fall through. I can't tour again. "Wait. Let me look over the budget. Maybe I can cut some things. Raise...some of the prices."

"Very well. Send me your new proposal within the week."

"I will."

She hangs up. I lay in bed another few minutes wishing the day had started differently. Vi's already gone when I pull my tired ass out of bed, shit, shave and shower and grab coffee.

The kitchen table is covered with the new puzzle I bought Vi, and I smile and try to put two pieces together. Ten minutes later I realize this is not something I'll be doing without Vi by my side, so I shuffle a few pieces around to make it look like I accomplished something, and I take my laptop and coffee to the coffee table to work. But it's not happening. The living room is messy. Dirty clothes scattered around. Empty dishes sitting out.

I take twenty minutes to clean up, do dishes and run a vacuum through the place. I look around and nod. That's better.

I sit back down and realize I'm hungry, so I rummage through the kitchen until I find an apple and some peanut butter. I take my time eating, knowing I'm procrastinating. Knowing I don't want to do this shit, but I must if the youth center has any chance of success. Once I'm fed, hydrated, the house is clean and I have no other distractions to justify stalling, I sit back down and look over my plans.

There are things I can do to increase the profit margin... if I let go of my morals and the reason I'm starting this center to begin with. I compromise. I raise prices, but also raise extra funding for those who qualify. I look for other ways to cut corners in the budget. It's mind-numbing work. Midway through the day I stop for a quick lunch of chicken salad and a green drink and then dive back into it. By evening, I've trimmed a couple grand off the business costs. I don't know if it's enough. It'll have to be.

I email Mrs. Wallace the new proposal, head out to pick up some groceries, and drive to Kevin's.

When I arrive, Mary says he's out with friends. I help her cook a stew for dinner.

"How are things with the center?" she asks.

"Fine. How are things with work?"

"Fine."

We've both learned to keep our sorrows close. We don't talk of troubles.

Kevin returns just as dinner is ready, bounding through the house with all the enthusiasm of youth. "Lach, dude, glad you're here."

I high five him. "You too, buddy. How's it going?"

He shrugs. "Same old. Starving though. Let's eat!"

Mary laughs, Kevin sets the table with some prompting and the three of us settle into our seats and count off the things we're grateful for. New on my list is Vi.

"You've got a girlfriend?" Kevin asks, his face a comical cross between grossed out and impressed.

"Looks like it," I say. "Tomorrow morning is our first date."

"Where are you two going?" Mary asks between bites.

"It's a surprise."

I tell them my plans and even Kevin is impressed.

They wish me luck as I leave, and I'm no longer worrying about money and investors. Our super secret date will be soon. Now all I need is a blindfold.

ELEVEN

Vi

I stare at the blindfold as if it's a poisonous snake intent on biting me. "Seriously?"

He grins. "Seriously. It's a surprise. You have to be blindfolded. Besides, what better way to begin this budding romance but with a game of trust?"

"Fine, you want trust? You wear the blindfold." I hold the black silk out to him but he doesn't accept it.

"I could, but I'm not sure you want me driving while blindfolded."

"I'm perfectly capable of driving," I tell him. We're standing by the front door and were just about to leave for our first date when he sprung the blindfold on me.

"But you don't know where we're going."

"You could tell me, and then all of this would be moot."

"And the fun would be spoiled. Come on, Vi. Let those impenetrable walls down a bit and have some fun. I promise, I won't break you." He takes the blindfold from my hand and lifts it to my eyes.

I have to make a choice. Surrender to him, or ruin our first date before it's begun?

This wouldn't be a hard choice for most people—but then I'm not most people, I guess. Still…I'm loath to ruin what might be just because it's hard to relinquish control.

So, I do it again. I surrender. I close my eyes, and he ties the silk around my eyes and leads me to his car, the cold morning air nipping at my exposed flesh.

It's unnerving, trusting someone to guide me. I'm usually the one putting on the blindfold, not wearing it. But excitement builds for this unusual date as he drives us to our destination in the still dark morning, made darker by the black silk over my eyes.

"What kind of date has to happen before the crack of dawn?" I ask, yawning. I'm not the best morning person in the world. Fortunately for Lach's sake, he had coffee ready before waking me up for this experience.

"The kind that's a surprise," he says. "Did no one ever explain the concept of a surprise to you?"

"I'm familiar with it in theory, but I prefer to know ahead of time what's happening with my life. I've never been a huge fan of surprises. I find anticipation is more exciting than surprise. If I know what's going to happen I can look forward to it, think about it, imagine it. A surprise leaves nothing but shock. It's not worth it." I sip at my coffee, carefully navigating it to my mouth so I don't spill it everywhere.

"We're going to have to work on this. I can't accept a *no-surprise* clause to our relationship along with everything else."

I swallow my argument along with the last dregs of sugary sweet liquid as he slows the car to a stop.

"We're here!" He sounds like a kid about to open their birthday present, and it's endearing in an unexpected way. And almost makes me excited about a surprise.

I grin, and pull my leather jacket around my body as he guides me out of the car and into the still cold morning. "When do I get to actually see this date?" I ask. "Please tell me I don't have to do the whole thing blind. I'm not sure I can handle that."

He laughs, and I enjoy the deep timbre of it. "Soon, babe. Soon, you will see everything."

My arm is linked into his, the warmth of his body filling me as we walk the few feet to this mystery date. When he breaks contact to take my blindfold off, I'm surprised to immediately miss the feel of him.

"Ready?"

I would glare at him, but he can't see my eyes, so I stick my tongue out instead. So mature, I know, but the teasing is fun, if juvenile. This is something new for me. I'm not used to being so…relaxed? Fun? I don't know the word, but there's a sense with Lachlan that I don't have to be in control all the time. That I can actually let my guard down and be silly. It's a bit disconcerting, but not in a bad way.

His hand brushes against my cheek as he unties the black silk. When my eyes open, it takes a moment to adjust to the still mostly dark sky, but then I see where we are and my heart does a little leap.

Before us a man is spreading out a yellow and orange tent of material attached to a large basket. Goosebumps cover my arms as all the pieces come together. "We're going hot air ballooning?"

"Yes." I can tell he's waiting to see if this is good for me or not, and in an out-of-character display of physical enthusiasm I throw myself into his arms.

He's quick to respond, his arms tightening around my waist as our bodies press together, my lips finding his before

I have time to think. His lips are soft and his kiss is the perfect mix of slow and teasing that builds into something more. Passionate, probing, full of sexual desire. We're interrupted by the man behind us clearing his throat.

"We're all set," he says, and Lachlan pulls away and introduces us.

"Vi, this is Clint, an old buddy of mine who gives the occasional tour via hot air balloon to tourists."

I hold out my hand and accept his handshake. He's not as tall as Lachlan, and not as athletically built, but he's got a kind face and a welcoming smile. He reminds me a bit of a farmer in a fairy tale, with his flannel and jeans and bearded face, and his hands are calloused, like someone who works hard with them.

"Nice to meet you, Clint. What do you do when you're not doing this?"

"I train horses," he says.

Lachlan pats Clint's back. "He's a jack-of-all-trades and was kind enough to set up a private balloon ride for us."

"Have you ever been?" Clint asks me.

"No, but I've always wanted to. I recently went skydiving for the first time. I loved it." I grin at Lachlan. "You pretty much nailed my first date fantasy, by the way. Horseback riding would have been a close second."

He takes a dramatic bow. "Glad to be of service to milady. Would you say this was worth a surprise?"

I purse my lips and try not to smile so broadly my face cracks. "I suppose you get a pass on the no-surprise clause for this one."

He slips an arm around my shoulder and leans in. "I still haven't agreed to that one, and am not likely to. I have many surprises planned for you, babe. And you'll love them all."

My knees quiver a bit at the implied promises his voice holds.

Clint is already turned away from us, prepping the balloon. We watch in silence as it fills with air, expanding larger than I imagined it would until there's space for us to enter the basket.

"We can accommodate a much larger group," Clint says as we enter the basket. "But Lachlan made it clear this needed to be a private party."

Once inside, I expect to feel a jolt, a sudden lurch from the earth as we became airborne. Instead, I'm caught up in a dreamlike flotation that lifts us from one plane of existence and into the heavens. I hold my breath and lean against the side to take in everything. The sun is starting to rise, filling the sky with the brightening hues of pinks, yellows, oranges and reds. Lachlan comes up behind me and embraces me, his arms reaching around to grip the edge of the basket on either side of me as we soar higher and higher over Nevada.

Clint leaves us to our own world, and it's easy to forget he's even there as we glide gently along, the humming of the fires giving us occasional lift. The movement through the sky is exhilarating, and my heart pings a new rhythm of happiness as I enjoy this moment with Lach's arms around me.

He leans in, his lips brushing my ear. "You're stunning when you smile," he says.

I turn in his arms, facing him instead of the vista before me. He's just about as breathtaking as the view. "You've outdone yourself. I fear you've set up our relationship to fail, though," I tease, my hands on his muscular chest.

"How so?" he furrows his brow in mock-worry.

"What could compete with this? You should have started small. Halfway decent pizza with some live music that didn't quite suck. Work your way up to the magical. But now, you've blown your wad on the best date ever. We have nowhere to go from here but down." I twist to look below us. "Literally."

He laughs. "Babe, if you think I've blown my wad..." he presses his hips into me, and I feel his hard cock throbbing beneath his jeans, "...then you don't know me very well."

"That's true," I admit. "I don't know you well. This is, after all, only our first date."

He grazes my cheek with his long fingers and smiles down at me. "The first of many."

We spend an hour in the sky, and before we get ready to descend, Lachlan pulls two flutes and a bottle of champagne from his bag. He pops the cork and pours our drinks. "To us," he says.

We clink glasses, and I sip the bubbly drink as the last of the darkness is pushed away by the sun.

. . .

I'm reluctant to leave the otherworldly magic of the balloon. Lachlan grins and reaches for my hand, leading me back to the car. I turn and wave at Clint. "Thank you," I say. "This was amazing."

He smiles back at us. "Glad to help! You should come see the horses some time."

I nudge Lachlan and grin. "Thank you too, for this most amazing date."

"You're very welcome. Thanks for trusting me." He stops and caresses my face. "I know it's not easy for you, and I appreciate it."

His words melt me and by the time we arrive home, I'm horny. I want him bad. But he *tsk*s me. "You have work, and this is only our first date. We have two more before sex can happen, remember?"

I groan. "You were serious? You of the perpetual one night stand? Seriously?"

He kisses my forehead. "Babe, you're not one of my perpetual one night stands. That's the point."

"Fine," I say, pulling away with a grin. "But I get to plan the next date. And I know just the thing."

He raises an eyebrow. "Very well, mistress. I'm open to being wooed by my woman. When shall I be ready?"

"Tomorrow night," I say with a smirk. Because that third date needs to happen.

Fast.

TWELVE

Lach

Paintball. That's Vi's idea for our next date. So I'm dressed in camouflage. Not sure if the designer was trying to create clothing or an oven, because I'm slick with sweat. My head's covered in a helmet that recreates the experience of being blind. It makes breathing hard. I feel like Darth Vader.

Vi's dressed the same, but the uniform hugs her curves in just the right way. I wish I could see her better. She shows me how to load my gun with paintballs. There's so many colors, I feel like I'm about to shoot people with skittles.

She escorts me out of the office building and into the arena. It's a giant pit of sand covered in sporadic blocks and hollow houses. The sun is bright. It burns my eyes and destroys the remaining bits of vision I have left. That's fine. I don't need to see, right? There are a few dozen people with us. No way I'm fucking counting them. The supervisor divides us into two teams. Reds and blues. Vi and I are red. The supervisor goes over the rules. All I remember is, if you're shot in the torso or head, you're out. Before the battle starts, we're allowed to take positions on opposite sides of the arena. Vi and I hide out in a one-story bunker.

"How do we win?" I ask.

Her voice is muffled. "We kill them all."

"Great. So, how do we do that?"

She points at a building near the center of the arena. "We advance to that bunker. From there, we shoot everyone."

"Sounds simple."

Vi scoots toward a window. "You go first. I'll cover you."

I'm reminded of a war movie. "I can't leave you behind."

"I'm the better shot. I'll be fine."

She's got a point. I have no idea how to shoot. "Fine. I'm going."

Vi nods. "Ready. Set. Go."

I turn a corner and charge toward a bunker, yelling at the top of my lungs. Things whoosh through the air. I assume people are firing at me. I hear Vi yell behind me. "You shoot at my man? Take this, you motherfuckers!" And I may be imagining this, but I feel like her voice sounds more and more like Arnold Schwarzenegger by the second.

"Lach, get down!" Okay. That one was like a perfect Arnold impression. I'm almost waiting for her to tell me to "get to the chopper!"

I dive forward, landing in the bunker. Sand shoots up around me. Some gets in my mouth. Helmet, what the fuck are you good for?

As I climb further into the bunker, something bites my leg. What the fuck? Snakes? Vi did not tell me there would be snakes. Wait…I notice the yellow paint on my foot. Someone shot me. Motherfucker. It hurts. I massage my foot.

A shadow fills the doorway. What the—

The enemy jumps out a few feet in front of me. I close my eyes and fire.

"Lach. Lach, it's me."

I stop firing and open my eyes. Vi stands in the doorway, a rainbow of colors around her. I sigh in relief. "Sorry, babe."

"It's okay. It's your first time. At least you got to the bunker."

"I did, didn't I? Sorry for shooting you...Wait. There's no paint on you. You were like four feet away."

"Yeah. Your aim sucks."

I couldn't hit her from four feet away.

I.

AM.

FUCKING.

DOOMED.

Vi pats me on the shoulder. "Lach, you okay?"

"Yeah. Sure. Why?"

"You sound like you need an inhaler."

I chuckle. "It's the helmet."

She sits beside me under a window. "Okay. Now, stick your head out. Tell me how many people are in that next building."

"Why do I stick my head out?"

"You're less valuable."

Can't argue with that. I stick my head out. There's one, two...oh yeah, I can't fucking see. I lower my head. "There's like four guys."

Vi smacks me on the helmet. "Like four guys, or four guys?"

"I don't know. I just saw blobs of darkness."

"Okay. I'll take care of it." She stands and starts firing. I get a blurry view of her ass. It inspires me to keep going.

Something hits my hand. It goes numb. "Fuck!"

Vi sits back down, hiding behind the wall. "What happened?"

I show her my hand. "It's bleeding."

"That's red paint."

Oh. It does not feel like red paint. And if you think it can't possibly hurt that much, then let me shoot your hand with a Skittle of Evil. You. Will. Cry.

Not that *I'm* crying, that is. Just…just shut the fuck up.

"Pay more attention," says Vi.

"It'll be a lot easier if you weren't so distracting."

"Oh, so it's my fault you got shot."

I smile. "Exactly."

Though I can't see her face, I imagine her smiling back. She raises her gun and shoots my other hand.

"What the fuck?"

"*Now* it is my fault you got shot. Want to blame me again?"

"Nope. I'm good." I flex my hands, trying to regain feeling. It doesn't work. "So, what's next?"

Vi looks out the window and then ducks her head back in. "Fuck. We're surrounded."

"It's the end, isn't it?"

She makes a fist. "We can't give up."

"What can we do?"

"Wait. Then die." She pulls off her helmet and frowns.

My jaw falls. "We can take our helmets off?"

"No. But who'll see?"

She's got a point. I rip my helmet off. Vision returns. I can breathe again. When I tell my children my favorite memories, this will be among them. Breathing.

I toss the vile thing aside. "Well, since the world is about to end, we might as well make the best of it."

Vi bites her lip. "What do you have in mind?"

I drop my gun and grab her waist. I press my lips against hers. "I need you, Vi."

"Lach. We can't."

I cup her ass. "We may never get another chance."

Her hand trails down my chest. Lower, lower. She stops. "No. We can't. People are counting on us."

"What people?"

She pulls away. "Our teammates. They need us." She shrugs. "Well, they need *me*."

"But—"

"No. Get your helmet back on. Besides, we're only on date two, remember?"

I grit my teeth and do it. Just one more date, Lach. Just one more date.

Vi puts on her helmet and grabs both guns. "I'll take the motherfuckers out. You'll help."

I yank on her uniform. "How can I help without a gun?"

She pauses. "A lot more than *with* a gun."

She's got a point. "What should I do?"

"Run out and distract them. I'll use you as a human shield."

I raise a finger. Before I can object, she shoves me out of the bunker.

Oh fuck.

I charge with my hands out. Paintballs swish around me. I think I see a box to hide behind. I dash forward. And then I am hit where no man should ever feel pain.

I collapse behind the box. Tears pour from my eyes. I feel like fireworks are going off in my balls.

Vi takes cover beside me. "What happened…Oh my God. Didn't you rent a cup?"

I spit as I talk. "I thought I'd save on the discomfort."

"Yeah. You look really comfortable."

"Fuck. Vi." I pull her closer. "I'm not gonna make it."

"Hang in there, stud."

"Tell my balls that." The pain builds. I can't take it anymore. My limbs go limp. I lie lifeless on the sand.

Vi screams at the heavens. Then she leans downs and whispers. "I will avenge you."

I see her blurry form jump up and unleash the Skittles of Evil. Blobs of darkness collapse under her assault. She is vengeance incarnate. She is death.

My cock starts to get hard before her beautiful display. Oh fuck, that's not a good idea. Not when your testicles have been replaced with bowling balls on fire. I squeeze my thighs together to stop the erection. Thank God I googled this shit.

Vi spins in a circle. A tornado of rainbows and death. And then she freezes. She collapses. Her voice is half a sob. "Oh God. The paint got in my mouth." It's all over her helmet.

With my last breath, I crawl toward her. I grab her hand. Darkness comes for me…

Because I can barely see shit.

Cheers erupt all around us. Someone announces. "Blue team is victorious!"

We pull off our helmets, and I help Vi stand up. "We did our best," I say.

She puts a hand to her mouth. "This is so disgusting. Fucking helmet." She stares at it as if it betrayed her. "You had *one* job, helmet. You failed."

The blue team members around us remove their helmets. They're pretty short. One guy has braces. We lost to a bunch of tweens? As we limp out of the arena, I nudge Vi on the shoulder. "Let's never speak of this, okay?" I say.

She laughs. "You never speak of it. I'm telling everyone how you got shot in the balls."

THIRTEEN

Vi

Lachlan insists on planning our third date and once again makes it a surprise. I'm pretty sure this man is trying to kill me with happiness. And, surprisingly, I'm okay with that.

In fact, he doesn't even tell me when the date is happening. I stumble upon it coming home from work two days after our paintball war and a day before my birthday. And yes, things happened in my normal everyday life in those two days. But do you really want to hear about me getting an oil change or balancing the accounts at Whipped or how I ate too many cupcakes when one of our vendors brought them to the shop and I spent all afternoon whining to Zoe about it? I didn't think so. Dates with Lachlan, and especially the *third* date with Lachlan, are way more interesting.

It's Friday night. I don't have plans specifically, but I assume my evening will involve Lachlan in some capacity, since every evening this week has. Though sadly it has not involved his cock since the night at his show. But that shit better be changing soon. Because *third date!*

So I'm expecting *something* tonight. Just not this.

This is my entire apartment covered in sheets when I open the door. "Lachlan?" I'm afraid to take a step inside. I'm not even sure there's a spot I can actually step into. Multi-colored sheets, including the ones from my bed, are pinned to the walls and draped over furniture as the edges fall to the floor in different patterns.

"Hey, babe!" I hear his voice through the curtain of cotton, but I can't see him. "You have to get on your hands and knees," he says, as if this explains everything.

"What are you talking about? What is this?"

His head pops out from below one of the sheets near me, a big grin on his handsome face. I gasp and jump. "Haven't you ever built a fort from sheets before?"

I shake my head, heart rate still high from the sudden appearance of his face. "Nope. Never."

He holds a hand up to me, and I drop my purse by the door, kick off my red stiletto heels and sink to my knees, accepting his hand as he draws me into the world he created with our bedding.

"You're missing out," he says. "This is a rite of passage for any child, but it takes on a different energy as an adult. I've created a labyrinth of rooms, each containing a tease for your senses and culminating in the final surprise of the night. You must experience each room fully before progressing to the next. Understand?"

"I think so." But I'm regretting my choice of attire for the day. Namely, the black leather mini-skirt that makes crawling on my hands and knees less than comfortable.

He smirks when he sees me tugging on my skirt. "It's time for the first tease," he says, leading me over to a white box with a giant red bow. "This is for you."

"Presents!" I may not like surprises, but I *love* presents. My excitement is palpable as I open up the box, and I sigh in delight at the contents. It's a beautiful silk nightgown in jewel tones of red, purple and emerald green. "Oh, Lachlan, this is gorgeous. Thank you so much!"

He makes a pretense of covering his eyes. "You must change into it before we can proceed to the next room."

Grateful to relieve myself of the clothing I'm wearing, I quickly change into the new nightgown. It's like wearing a cloud. I feel sexy and alluring in it, my shoulders bare and the plunging neckline accentuating my best features. The top of the sheet tent brushes against my head as I kneel before Lachlan. He has to slouch not to burst out of it entirely. I'm guessing these tents are easier for children to navigate, but it's still fun.

He runs a hand over my shoulders and slides a finger down my neckline, our eyes locked in heated anticipation. "What do we do now?" I ask, hoping I won't need the nightgown for long.

"Now, we move to the next room and see what awaits us." He points to a pillowcase hanging from the sheet. I assume it's meant to be a door, and I crawl through it and am greeted by a picnic of delectable desserts spread out on the rug with brightly colored pillows arranged artfully around the feast.

Lachlan positions himself over a few of the pillows, resting on his elbow, so I do the same, facing him. He holds up that black silk blindfold, and I moan. "Again?"

He nods and ties it around my eyes. "For this tease, you must focus on your other senses while I feed you."

This exercise is unbelievably sensual as I open my mouth and he places a small bite of something sweet. I savor the melting chocolate with a hint of mint, letting the taste fill me. Next is a strawberry dipped in more chocolate, and then he holds a glass to my lips, and I sip champagne. Next comes something salty. Oyster. An aphrodisiac. I smile as I let the cool salty bite slide down my throat.

When his lips touch mine, I'm ready to take him in. To taste him and feel him and fuck him so very hard, but he pulls away as my body aches for more. "Not yet," he whispers, slipping the blindfold off me. "One more room."

I crawl through another pillowcase and into a kaleidoscope of color. Soft music begins playing and this room is entirely covered by floor pillows and soft blankets. Colorful Christmas lights are strung from every possible location, making the whole room feel like a magical land in another world.

Lachlan kisses me again, deeply this time, urgently, and lays me back on the pillows, positioning himself over me. "We've come to the end of our third date, Vi."

"So we have," I say, gazing intently into his too-blue eyes.

"And now, I'm going to make love to you like you've never been made love to in your life."

My body shivers with the promise as his lips fall to my neck. I feel his breath as he whispers. "After tonight, you will be mine, and I will be yours."

His words scare and excite me in equal measure. He's claiming me with every breath, with every touch, with every romantic gesture. And in the process, he's changing me. I feel the shift—slow, nearly imperceptible, but *there* nonetheless.

I'm not the same Vi I was before I met him.

But I can't think too deeply about these things because this gorgeous man is sliding his hand up my thigh and over the silk panties I'm wearing. His thumb brushes against my pussy through the thin fabric, teasing without giving me any real satisfaction, as he uses his other hand to bring my wrist to his mouth. With gentle pressure, he kisses the inside of my wrist, then bares his teeth, letting them skim across the tender flesh. I moan in unexpected pleasure at his expert teasing of an often-ignored erogenous zone.

I'm ready to be naked and spread before him, but he has other plans. He's intent on building up the tension in me to excruciating degrees. Letting go of my wrist, his mouth finds my collarbone, trailing soft brushes of his lips down my chest, flicking a tongue over a hard nipple through my nightgown, his hands now gripping my hips. I gasp. "Lachlan, you're killing me."

He looks up, a sly grin on his lips. "Babe, you ain't seen nothing yet."

Turns out, he's right. As he works his way down my body—so very slowly—he finds spots to tease and torture that no man ever explored before.

"Turn over, babe. And take off your clothes. All of them."

"This seems imbalanced. You're still in jeans and a shirt."

"I'll be naked soon enough. Now turn over. Trust me. You want to do what I tell you."

I peel off my nightgown before I turn over, giving him a full few of my breasts. His breath hitches, and I smile teasingly and shimmy out of my underwear, giving him glimpses between my legs as I do. If he's going to torture me, I want him to feel the pain too.

When I finally lay on my stomach, the soft blankets cushioning my naked skin, my body coils in increased tension. I don't know what he's going to do. I'm not in control. I'm not the one wielding the power. It scares me. And excites me. I breathe deeply, trying to relax as I anticipate what he might do.

He starts gently, hands running over my shoulders, my back, down to my ass. First with a light tickling of his fingertips. The contact sends shivers over my body. When he increases the pressure, gripping my ass harder as he massages me, I moan. His hands feel amazing, and my hips naturally arc into them, greedy for more.

He lightens his touch again as his hands run down my legs, stopping behind my knees. Then I feel his warm breath against my skin, followed by the gentle touch of his lips as he caresses the skin. I know this is a sensitive spot for women, but I've never had anyone explore my body this way. I'm hooked on how it feels. When his tongue flicks out, teasing my flesh, I moan, my leg flexing in reflex.

He works his way down my calves to my feet, rubbing, massaging, bringing pleasure to every inch of my body.

When he moves back up my legs and places his hands over my ass, spreading my legs until I'm fully exposed to him, I begin to shake from need.

He lifts my hips with strong hands, and then his tongue teases my pussy from behind. The erotically-charged position and act nearly sends me over the edge, but he stops before I can come.

"Not yet, babe. Let it build." His voice is husky, and I can tell he's exercising a lot of self-control as well.

The knowledge brings me pleasure. "Someday it'll be your cock in my mouth, and I'll remember this."

He laughs. "I certainly hope so."

And then he is silent, his mouth once again working magic between my legs, hands gripping my ass. He takes me to the edge over and over, stopping before I can fall. I want to fall. I want to fall so fucking bad.

He flips me over then, my body still quivering with how close I am to coming. While I watch, he strips off his shirt, exposing a body sculptured from marble and the wet dreams of every woman alive.

When he pulls off his pants I nearly come without his touch. He is huge. Hard. Glorious.

"I want you to come on my cock, babe. And then I want to fuck you all night long." He slips on a condom, and I spread my legs.

Oh God. Yes. With one hard thrust, he is deep inside me, and I am coming hard, flung off the side of that particular mountain in an instant. My body clenches, muscles spasming in final blissful release. He holds himself still inside of me for a moment and then thrusts deeply, repeatedly, holding my hips as he fucks me the way I've been dreaming he would since the night in his dressing room.

He is true to his promise. We break for water, for food, for making out and holding each other, but then we fuck again. In every position, in all the rooms of our tent house, slowly, quickly, passionately and tenderly. I lose count of my orgasms, and his. I lose count of everything but the feel of our flesh connected, of his scent and taste and the way he fills me and touches me and makes me feel.

And it is exquisite.

At the break of dawn we finally rest, my head against his chest, his arms around me, and that is how I fall asleep and wake up.

And, I realize, this is the best birthday present I could have asked for.

...

The next day Lachlan asks me to join him for the day. "I want to show you what I'm really about."

His comment intrigues me, and after we pull down the fort of sheets and put everything away, I follow him out for a Saturday adventure that could involve anything.

Given his regular job, I couldn't be more shocked when we arrive at a low-income neighborhood to pick up three kids.

Two boys and a girl stand around a basketball court waiting. When Lachlan and I walk up, one of the boys runs up to him, a big grin on his face. "Dude, you're late."

"Sorry, Kev, I overslept a bit. I'd like you to meet someone."

They both turn to me, and I hold out my hand. "Hi, I'm Vi."

The boy takes my hand and gives Lachlan a big grin. "Is this the chick you've been mooning over?"

I laugh as we shake, and Lach nudges the kid. "This is Kevin and his friends Mike and Lauren. I've been teaching them dance after school."

The kids follow us back to the car and climb in. "Where are we going now?" I ask.

"I'm going to show you my dream."

We arrive at the old mall and park in front of it. "I want to turn this into an after-school program for dance, free to any kid who needs a safe place to go after school and wants to learn dance, do homework, hang out."

I whistle under my breath. "I had no idea."

"I know what it's like to be on your own too young. I want these kids to have someone."

We get out and walk around as he describes what he envisions everywhere. The stage, the rooms for rehearsals, a game room and study room. He dreams big, and I fall a little harder for him because of it.

Several hours have passed when we get back and drop the kids off. We walk Kevin home and his mother greets us at the door. She smiles widely at Lachlan and then pulls me into a hug after introductions are made. "So nice to meet a friend of Lachlan's. He's such a dear man. Won't you two be staying for dinner? I've made plenty."

A quick look at their humble home was enough to tell me they probably didn't have 'plenty' to spare, but you'd never know it the way she opened her home to us. Again, I wondered at this man I was just getting to know. Who was he underneath all the sexy?

"Thank you, but we have other plans tonight," says Lach. "I promise I'll be by next week for your famous fried chicken, though. Wouldn't miss that." He kisses her cheek and we leave. On the way back from the car he reaches for my hand. "Thank you for coming today. It means a lot to share this with you."

I squeeze his hand, my heart swelling with a flurry of confusing emotions. "Thank you for bringing me."

"There's one more thing I'd like to show you, if that's okay?"

I nod. "Of course. I'm enjoying spending the day with you."

And it's probably good we aren't still at home. Because we'd both want more fucking and my pussy probably needs a brief reprieve to recuperate.

This time he takes me to a very different neighborhood. One of wealth and prestige, with huge houses meant for the rich. He stops in front of one of the nicest ones. "This is going to be my house, once all the paperwork is finalized."

I whistle under my breath. I knew he had money, but I didn't know it was this much. "It's gorgeous."

He nods. "I've wanted a house like this my whole life. I used to dream about it when I was a kid, living in a place like Kevin's. Only my mom didn't cook fried chicken or keep things clean. I had to fend for myself as she left empty bottles of booze and overflowing ashtrays everywhere. I was lucky if I got a hot meal even once a week. This was my dream. To live somewhere that would always be warm, clean, spacious and full of food."

My heart breaks for that little boy he was, and I want to kick his mother in the crotch for being so lousy. Instead, I hold his hand. "You deserve a house like this and a life like that," I say.

We drive home in silence. I haven't told him it's my birthday, and I'm not sure I will. This day has been perfect, and I wouldn't change anything about it.

Until we get to our front door.

When I open it, the dark living room explodes in a group of people jumping up to scream, "Happy birthday, Vi!"

I punch Lachlan in the arm. "A surprise party?"

He grins at me and pulls me closer to him, kissing me on the head. "You'll get used to the surprises, Vi. I promise. Happy birthday, babe."

FOURTEEN

Lach

Kacie and Tate know how to throw a party. I contacted them to plan something special for Vi, and they turned our apartment into a dance club. The lights are low. A disco ball hangs from the ceiling. Tate has a mini bar set up in the kitchen. Kacie manages a playlist of pop songs in the living room. People dance and drink all over.

I wrap my arms around Vi as we move to the music. "Never knew you had so many friends." I let Kacie and Tate handle most of the invites.

She grins. "I meet a lot of people at the store."

I notice a couple dry humping against a wall. "Really horny people."

"I do sell sex toys."

I twirl her around. "That reminds me. How'd you get into that?"

She shrugs. "I like sex. And I like helping people explore their sexuality. It's what I loved about being a Dominatrix."

"So why change careers?"

"Being a Dom made relationships...difficult. I never had sex with my clients, but they still found my sessions sexual. Intimate. Not a lot of guys could handle that."

I wonder if I could. I'm not sure. "Do you miss being a Dom?"

"Sometimes. I love how it forced me to be creative."

I frown. "Like painting?"

She laughs. "No. With my methods. Clients like variety. Every day, I had to discover new ways to blend pleasure and pain. I still get ideas, but..." she hesitates. "It's harder to try them."

I feel like she means impossible. I wonder if this is a problem. I'm not submissive. I take control. She seems to enjoy it, but she must miss being in charge. Could I enjoy letting go?

Vi kisses my cheek. "I need a drink. Want anything?"

I shake my head. She walks off toward the kitchen. I think our conversation soured her mood. Mental note. Don't bring up points of contention at girlfriend's birthday party.

Tate shuffles through the crowd and clasps my shoulder. "Hey, man. Having fun?"

"Yeah. Thanks for the help. When my buddies decide to tie the knot, and I should let you know it may be another ten years, I'm recommending you guys for the bachelor party."

"Nice." Tate sways his arms. "I...um...I liked your show."

I chuckle. "Vi told me you ended up there. Heard you kinda freaked out. For future reference, it's a great place to pick up women."

"Huh. Never thought about that." He sips a glass of orange liquid. "You must have met a lot of girls there."

"Yeah."

"A new girl each night."

I don't like where this is going. "My contract's almost up."

"Good." Tate's words are slurring. He's getting drunk. "Because you know, Vi's not a one night kind of girl."

"And I'm not a one night kind of guy. Not anymore. I insisted on three dates before sex."

His eyes go wide. "Three. Man, I'm not sure I could do that. Nice. Okay, listen, you seem nice. And you dance well. So, I won't get in your way. But if you break my girl's heart..." He makes a stick with his hands and pretends to break it.

I'm not sure he could actually take me. But it's a sweet sentiment.

"I have no intention of leaving her," I say firmly.

He nods. "Good. I'll get back to the bar. You get back to your girl."

As he wobbles away, Kacie walks up next to me, swiping her stylishly messy blond hair off her face. "He give you the Tate Test?"

Is this Vi's party? Or the Lachlan experiment? But hey, I never spent a lot of time with Vi's friends. I should have expected this. "I think so."

Kacie smiles. "He didn't hit you with a bottle of vodka. So that's a good sign."

I raise an eyebrow. "He's done that before?"

"He used to be the bouncer for all of our bachelor parties. A few times, things got wild."

I nudge her shoulder. "So is this the Kacie Test?"

"Yeah. But it's pretty simple." She changes her voice. It reminds me of someone from the Godfather movie. "You gonna be the perfect guy for my girl?"

"I'll do my best."

"Yay. Now, I have to go find Sebastian. The babies are with a sitter, and we're getting crazy tonight." She saunters away to her husband.

I glance around for Vi. Instead, I see Zoe running toward me, her purple bob bouncing with each step. Did they plan this?

I raise my hand, stopping Zoe in her tracks. "Vi's awesome. I have no intention of leaving her. I'll be the best boyfriend ever. Did I get everything?"

She gives me a thumbs-up and disappears back into the crowd. Am I drunk, or does she look like Tinkerbell?

The doorbell rings. How many friends does Vi have?

I open the door. A guy with blond hair stands in the doorway, guitar case in one hand, flowers in the other. "You here for the party?" I ask.

"Yeah. I'm Chad. I used to be Vi's boyfriend."

I grit my jaw. That unfamiliar feeling enters me again. "I don't think you're invited."

He smiles. "It's okay. I used to live here." He walks forward.

I stop him with my hand. "Well, Chad. I'm Lachlan. And I live here now."

The fucker's still smiling. "Vi would want to see me." He notices something behind my shoulder. "Hey! Vi, it's Chad."

I turn around. Vi walks up to us, a red glass in her hand. "Chad, what are you doing here?"

"I wanted to surprise you. Here, for you." He holds out the flowers.

Vi doesn't move. "Chad. You need to leave."

"Come on, Vi. We need to talk."

"We have talked. Goodbye, Chad."

Before he can protest, she closes the door on him. I don't know what I expected, but it wasn't this. I like it. "So that's your old boyfriend?"

She gulps down her drink. "Yeah. We lived together for a while. It was...You know what, I don't want to talk about it right now." Right. Don't bring up points of contention. Vi takes another sip. "I need a refill."

"I'll join you."

We walk over to the bar, and I order a Buttery Nipple. Yes, it's a drink. Vi orders a Miami Ice. Tate is a speed demon as he mixes the drinks. He passes us the glasses. "Here you go, guys. Sorry, but we're out of ice."

A thought crosses my mind. "I'll run out and get some."

Vi grabs my hand. "You sure?"

"Yeah. I'll go down to the corner store. I'll be just a minute."

She gives me a kiss. "Thanks."

I run out of the apartment. I pass a red bouquet on the stairs. I see Chad in the lobby and grab his shoulder. "You shouldn't have showed up."

"Get your hands off me, man."

I don't. I squeeze harder. "If Vi wants you to leave her alone, you leave her alone."

"She doesn't know what she wants."

I smirk. "Because she's not with you?"

"Because she's apparently with you, mister tough guy. She doesn't like that. Not really. She needs a sub." He sure *looks* like a sub. Small and thin. Pale. I imagine snapping him in two.

I lean closer and whisper in his ear. "If she really needed a sub, then she'd still be with you."

"Fuck you." He yanks my hand off and opens the door. He turns back for a moment. "Tell her happy birthday from me." He leaves.

I drive down to the corner store, buy a bag of ice, and return to the party. Tate mixes us more drinks. Vi caresses my face. "You okay? You're shaking?"

"Just tired. Happy birthday, babe."

But I'm not okay. We drink and dance and kiss, and Chad's words replay in my head. And I wonder if I *am* what Vi needs.

And if I'm not, if I can change.

FIFTEEN

Vi

The night of my birthday party, Lachlan and I fucked like we'd never fucked before. It was as if he had to prove how much he wanted me. I know seeing Chad there probably messed with him a bit. Honestly, it messed with me, too. Not that it made me doubt my feelings for Lach. But it was unsettling to consider how different I am with Lachlan compared to Chad.

Are both of those people me? Can I be just one side of that coin and still be happy?

It's been a lot to think about over the last few months, but it hasn't diminished the pleasure I've experienced being with Lachlan. It hasn't even bothered me that once he and his manager cooled off he was back at work turning women on.

I trust him, though. I know he's just performing. Just like it wasn't sexual with my clients when I was a Dom. I've given some thought to taking on a client or two, but it hasn't felt right. Not with Lach in my life. I understand why he's ready to leave the Aussie Posse. In addition to wanting to build something else with his life, it takes a lot of emotional and sexual energy to give people their fantasy day in and day out. Our jobs aren't so different.

But God, these last few months. I've become one of those people you avoid on Facebook because all my status updates are about how happy I am.

You'd think that after a few months of being with Lachlan every night, waking up to him every morning, fucking him every day—more than once—that the bloom would fade from the rose. That his tricks would wear thin and his cock would no longer be as satisfying.

You'd be dead wrong.

But.

BUT.

Routines happen, ya know? This is my home. I'm used to living alone. We haven't been a couple that long. And...did I mention I'm used to living alone?

I'm also used to being able to let my shit hang out at home. At work, both at Whipped and when I was a Dom, I have to be neat, orderly, all things in their place and in control. In my abode, I let my hair down and like things...casual.

Lachlan, surprisingly, is not quite as lackadaisical about his environment. Which he's making abundantly clear.

"Vi, babe, seriously? The laundry basket is literally less than a foot from the dirty clothes you dumped in the bathroom. Hon, I adore you to death, but really?"

He stands in the hall holding the wicker basket with a pained expression on his face.

I hold up my laptop as I slouch on the couch. "I'm about to level up on Diablo. I'll tidy up later."

"You always say later and later never happens."

"That's not true," I say as I kick some major spider ass with my badass magical powers. "Later just hasn't arrived yet.

You really stress out too much about the little things, my dear. Try to relax."

He drops the basket with so much drama I laugh as he scurries to the kitchen. "Something smells heavenly," I say. "What's for dinner?"

"Chickpea and potato curry with coconut sauce," he says from the other room.

"Oh my God, you are amazing."

He pokes his head out. "That's what she said."

I break from my game and throw a couch pillow at his him. "Ass."

He winks at me and ducks back into the kitchen. "You know babe, I don't have time to do all the cooking and the cleaning."

"Then don't clean." Seems reasonable enough to me. I mean, it's not like I let things get gross. They just get a bit... untidy. There *is* a difference, which is lost on Mr. Neat Freak.

"You know that's not a possibility," he says.

"I did offer to cook," I remind him as I finally level up.

He groans. "Yes. About that. I'm still recovering from the last time. I can't eat spaghetti and meatballs without feeling nauseous. I didn't know a person could screw up spaghetti."

"It's a gift," I tell him. I'm aware of my shortcomings when it comes to domestic life. That's what take-out is for. And why I'll never live in a small town where shit closes early and pizza is the only option. Nope, I'm a big city girl that runs 24/7 in all weather.

I'm lost in my next quest when Lachlan takes my computer away and pulls me off the couch. "I've just realized something."

"That you interrupted my game and got me killed?" I frown at him and reach for my computer but he blocks me with his delicious body.

"No. I realized why we've been bickering more lately."

"Why's that?"

"It's been more than twenty-four hours since we fucked."

I laugh. "And?"

"And that's obviously too long for us. It must be remedied, stat."

"Or what?"

He pulls me to him, tightening his grip around my waist. "You don't want to know the *or what*. Trust me."

And then he lifts me into his arms and carries me to my bedroom, which has become our bedroom in recent months.

I feign resisting, but I enjoy the teasing, the foreplay, the roughness as he throws me onto the bed and pulls off my pants. "I want you, Vi. Now."

"Then take me. If you can."

What ensues is an erotic wrestling match where he pushes my legs open, I fight him, there are love bites and a few playful slaps, and then I am on my knees, legs spread, as he pounds his cock into my eager pussy.

When he slaps my ass, the sting of it makes me so hot I come on his cock while he fucks me more.

And then I come again when he comes, both of us sweaty, out of breath, and satiated. For now.

In his arms, I sigh, snuggling closer, enjoying the scent of his body and the feel of his muscles under my hands.

He nuzzles my hair and kisses my head, and I can feel his smile as he says, "I think we leveled up."

SIXTEEN

Lach

My phone rings, and I wake. Come on. You don't call people this early. I mean it's only...oh, it's three in the afternoon. Give me a break. I had a late show last night.

I sit up in bed, sheets falling off my body, and look around. Vi is already gone to work, probably about seven hours ago. She was asleep when I got home last night. These hours suck for us both sometimes, but soon we'll have a schedule that matches. I'm looking forward to that.

My phone rings again and I remember why I'm even awake at all right now and check the caller ID. It's Mrs. Wallace. She must have looked over the revised proposal. I sent it months ago and have been on pins and needles waiting, but didn't want to appear overeager. Shit has to happen soon, though. My contract is nearly up and I have to make a decision. My stomach turns. I take deep breaths.

"Hello."

"Hello, Mr. Pierce. Tell me, did you understand our last conversation?"

I swallow, and it feels like I'm swallowing a rock. "Yes."

"Oh, then perhaps you need to brush up on your math, because this center is still a waste of resources."

I squeeze the phone. "The center will do exactly what it's supposed to."

"Except make money." She sighs. "I'm sorry, but I can't invest in your business. Good luck, Mr.—"

"Wait. Wait—"

The line goes dead. The conversation is over. My funding is gone.

I sit there, unable to fully grasp what just happened. I've been working on this deal for months. I've busted my ass, kissed other people's asses, done everything I could to make this dream real...and it all just disappeared because of one phone call. I realize my hand is gripping the phone so hard I might break it, so I put it down and take a few deep breaths to calm myself.

This is for the best. It has to be.

And maybe I'll eventually believe that.

I hear our front door open, which snaps me out of my pity party. I pull on a pair of jeans and walk into the living room. Vi's holding two paper cups. Her hair's up in a twist. "Brought you coffee, sleepy head."

"Thanks. No work?" I ask as I accept the cup and take a yummy sip.

"I opened. Zoe is closing." She tilts her head and frowns. "You okay? You seem...off."

I take another sip of my coffee and my head clears a bit, senses sharpening. Maybe it's just the placebo effect, but it works. I notice Vi's red shirt, tight over her breasts. I notice her shorts and her smooth legs. I take her coffee and set both down. I don't think. I act.

I wrap my arms around her. I kiss her. I push her back. I pin her against the door.

She moans. "Want to go to the bedroom?"

I bite on her neck. "No."

"The floor?"

"No. I need you *now*, Vi. I need my cock inside you." I unzip my pants and slip on a condom. I pull down her shorts and panties, and lift her up against the door. She wraps her legs around me.

And I slam my cock inside her. She feels soft and warm, and I need more. I start to pound her hard and fast, her back thudding against the door with each thrust. She runs her nails down my shoulders. She grabs my ass and pulls me closer, deeper. "Lachlan," she pants, her words made staccato by my movements, "don't stop."

I'm not about to. I have a hunger in me, and only Vi can quench it. "Where next? The floor? The couch?"

She bites her lip. "No. Don't stop."

"I won't." I swing away from the door, still holding her on my cock, and walk over to the couch. I drop her down on the cushions and pull her feet over my shoulders. She slips up her shirt, exposing her hard nipples. Fuck, she looks beautiful spread out before me. I start moving my cock again, more slowly this time, enjoying the view, enjoying the firm grip of her pussy.

She squeezes her tits together, playing with them. "Impressive," she says. "But you've slowed down. Getting tired?"

I ram my cock inside her so hard she screams.

"Not even close." I pound her deeper, harder, faster, running my hand through her hair. I tug on it, gently at first.

Then harder. She gasps, and I know she's close to coming. I speed up.

"Lachlan, fuck, your cock feels so good." Her pussy tightens, and she trembles with ecstasy in my arms. When she comes, we both cry out in pleasure. It's amazing. I'm not done.

I lift her up again and carry her to the kitchen table. She lays down flat over our shared puzzle. I spread her legs further than before, and slide my cock deep inside her. I feel her taking me in completely.

"Fuck, Lachlan. You feel so fucking huge."

This position does that. "I need you to feel all of me, Vi. I need you to understand how much I love your pussy. How much I need it."

"Yes. Show me."

I pull her legs in front of my chest and slightly cross them, creating a tighter fit for both of us. I begin to increase my speed. With one hand, I play with her tits. She grabs it and bites down on my fingers. Fuck. I let her moan on my fingers as I take her faster than ever, building toward a climax for us both. When she screams my name, I let myself go, coming inside her, falling down from a high that should never end.

I collapse on top of her, and we hold each other.

Vi smiles. "That was different."

"I needed different."

She teases. "Growing tired of me?"

I kiss her nose and pull away, zipping up my jeans. "Never."

"Good." She sits on the table. "Pass my pants." I throw them. She catches. "So, what happened?"

I raise my eyebrow. "What do you mean?"

"Something made you angry. You fuck harder when you're angry."

Can't argue with that. "My investor pulled out."

"I see, so in retribution you fucked me and didn't pull out once." She laughs for moment. I don't. She stops. "Sorry. That was...sorry." She stands up and grabs her coffee from the counter. "What are you going to do?"

"Find more investors and..." Fuck, who am I kidding? I've already looked. Mrs. Wallace was the only one interested. Apparently, because she misunderstood my goals. Of course, I haven't tried outside of Nevada, but that will take time. I've already spent enough.

"There is one option. I've been offered to tour one more year for two million." The words hurt to say.

Vi freezes, cup halfway to her mouth. "That's a lot of money. Where would you be going?"

"New York. Florida. All over the States."

"If you can't be here, that changes things."

I walk over to her. "I know. I haven't committed to anything yet."

She shrugs. "You should really think about it. Don't let what's going on between us stop you." She acts indifferent, but her body trembles.

I grab her hand. "It's too late for that. You're a part of my decisions now. I can't pretend like this relationship doesn't matter."

"Then don't, but don't give up your dreams for me."

Dreams? I used to have only one. Helping kids. But now, I have Vi. She snuck inside my picture of the future. She made it more messy and beautiful at once. I wouldn't have it change.

I lock up thoughts of money and business, and turn my attention to something I've been considering. "I ran into Chad the night of the party."

Vi drops her jaw. "Did you have to google how to hide a body?"

I chuckle. "No. We had a good talk. Well, a talk anyway. It got me thinking. We have an amazing sex life—"

"But…" She frowns.

I smile to put her at ease. "But I want to do more things you enjoy, try out the ideas you have. So if you need to do your thing with me…" I brush her cheek with my hand. "I once told you, there might be more pieces to you than you know. I now realize, there might be more pieces to me, too. I'll never know unless I try."

SEVENTEEN

Vi

I don't want Lach to leave. But I don't want to tell him to stay. Because I don't want to be the woman who ruins her lover's life by getting him to give up his dreams for her. Or something like that.

I'm really trying not to think about it.

It hurts too much. It scares me. Which is why tonight is the perfect time to be the Mistress again. And why I'm so grateful that Lachlan suggested this. Not that what we have in bed—and really on any surface we can find—hasn't been completely, unbelievably mind-blowing. It has.

But this is who I am too, and I can't give this up entirely, even for Lach.

So I'm ready. When he gets home everything will be set up for a night of kink and bondage.

But first, the food. I'm going to prove to him I can carry my own weight in our roommate/relationship arrangement, and that I can follow instructions to make dinner.

Tonight I've made us homemade macaroni and cheese, baked, with a salad bar. Can't go wrong with that, right?

I greet him with a kiss when he comes home and guide him to the candlelit table I've set up for us. He raises an eyebrow. "This wasn't what I was expecting."

I sit across from him and put a cloth napkin on my lap. "Oh, this isn't the Dom part. This is the girlfriend date part. The Dom part comes after dinner. Wait until you see the bedroom."

He glances toward the hallway with a bemused expression and then turns back to me. "And you cooked?"

I nod.

"From scratch?"

I nod again.

He sniffs the plate. "Seems okay. Looks great. I'm... impressed," he says, as if he's asking a question.

"Hey now, I'm not totally useless in the kitchen. I just got distracted the night I made the pasta."

"Distracted? That's what you call dumping an entire jar of chili pepper into the sauce and burning the garlic bread to small black disks?"

"It's Cajun style." I sip my wine, take a bite of the salad and smile.

We eat in comfortable companionship as I ask him about his day and how the funding for the center is going.

"No progress to report, but I'm not giving up."

"I'm glad." I take a big bite of the mac and cheese. It doesn't taste like I think it should, but that's probably from using goat milk instead of cow. I had to improvise when I realized I bought the wrong jug at the store the other day.

As the candles burn down and we finish our dinner, I stand and lead him to the bedroom. "Once we enter this room, I am in control. You will call me Mistress and do as I say, no questions. Understood?"

He nods.

"Are you ready for this?" I don't want to break my boyfriend just for some kink, but I'm revved up and anxious to do this, so I hope he says yes, and I hope I believe him, because if I don't, we can't do it. That's always been my rule.

"Yes, Vi, I'm ready for this."

I believe him. "Go into the room and wait for me. I'll be there shortly."

While he waits, I change into my Dom uniform. Spiked red heels. Black leather mini-skirt and a black lace corset. And I bring the whip.

His eyes get big when I come in, and so does his cock. So far, so good.

Butterflies dance in my stomach as I tell him to take off his clothes and then handcuff him to the bed. When I blindfold him, he smiles. "Turnabout's fair play," he says.

I gently lash his thigh with the leather whip. "Mistress," I remind him.

"Yes, Mistress."

"Good boy."

I straddle him and enjoy the feeling of being in control again. Though my mind flicks back to the nights he took me hard and fast, and I know he's changed me. I'll never be 'just' the Dom again.

And I realize I'm okay with that.

I tease him with feathers and whips, with teeth and tongue, tantalizing his senses as I take control of his body and make him beg for more.

It's exhilarating.

His cock is hard and throbbing when I finally mount him. I'm still wearing my black leather skirt, but it's more of a belt now, and there's nothing under it. I tease his tip with my wet pussy, taking him in just a bit, then pulling off, over and over, as he moans and tries to thrust his hips for more. I whip him again, lightly, but with a sting. "I'll give you more when I decide."

When he settles down, I drop my hips fully onto his cock, taking his shaft entirely. He fills me, stretches me, and I want more, but I want to torture him too. So I pull off and tease the tip again. I take off my corset and let my nipples fall against his lips. He's still blindfolded, but I can tell he's enjoying the extra play.

When neither of us can take it anymore, I give us both everything. Riding him hard and fast. Deeply, completely, until we both come.

I'm about to start it again, teasing, torturing, arousing him until he's hard once more, when my stomach rolls over, and I realize the butterflies I've been feeling aren't from nerves.

"Oh my God, I have to go!"

I run into the bathroom and can't even close the door before I'm vomiting all over the floor, the sink and finally into the toilet. I'm dying. Absolutely dying. Someone tried to kill me, and now I'm dying.

"Vi? You okay? What's going on?"

I can't talk yet, my stomach is still heaving everything I've ever eaten since I was two. When I catch a breath, I scream at him. "Sick. So sick. Oh God!"

What happened? How can I be sick so suddenly? I don't know and can't really think because now my stomach is out of food but is finding some kind of green sludge from the pits of despair and vomiting that up. I've never vomited this much. Ever.

"Vi! Vi? I think I'm getting sick too. Vi, you have to come release me."

Oh no. I can't leave him stuck to the bed. I try to move from the toilet, but another wave hits me, and I lean over, heaving until it hurts. "I'm trying, Lach. But I can't stop throwing up."

"Vi. I'm going to be sick."

And then I hear him vomit. All over my bed.

I crawl through my own sick to reach him, throwing up again on the floor. I scramble for the key to the handcuffs and get them off his wrists. He pulls the blindfold off and runs to the bathroom and vomits into the toilet. We are now both covered in each other's vomit.

It feels like hours before we're both done. We can't move and no longer care we are covered in sick.

We lean against the sink together, both of us slumped on the bathroom floor, when Lach starts to laugh.

I can't help but join in, because what else can you do but laugh or cry? And Lach chooses laughter, and I love that about him.

"Is this how it usually went with your clients?"

I laugh harder, my stomach cramping from it all. "Usually less vomit," I tell him. "But not always."

He chuckles. "Oh, Vi, honey…"

"Yes?"

"You're never allowed to cook."

EIGHTEEN

Lach

I'm not really the type to submit. But that night with Vi was hot—being tied up and tortured by her sexy ass and tits. Well, until the vomiting. That was the opposite of hot. But before then, I was down. And hard. So it hasn't been a hardship—pun intended—to play Master and Servant a few more times with her, under less spectacularly disgusting circumstances. It's not my thing 24/7, but for a change of pace, something new, I can get into the groove of being handcuffed and teased.

And I love seeing Vi light up when she's in charge. She's sexy as hell as a Dom, and I enjoy getting to know that side of her more than I imagined I would. We don't go too kink. Some of the stories she's told me, I know without trying that it's not for me. For example, I have zero desire to lick the bottoms of her heeled boots, no matter how sexy they are on her perfect little feet. So we have lines, and we learn as we play, and we give and take, and sometimes I'm holding the handcuff key, and sometimes she is. All in all, our sex life is even better for it, which is something I never thought I'd say. My sex life never seemed like it needed to be (or even could be) better. But there you have it. Learn something new every day.

So…we've been having fun. And somewhere in all that fucking and fun, shit got serious. I don't know when it happened. Whether it was the late nights watching sitcoms together and laughing at stupid jokes, or the weekend afternoons spent sorting laundry, or the petty bickering over whose turn it was to do the dishes (somehow it's never Vi's turn…) or maybe those long mornings spent in silence bent over a jigsaw puzzle together. I don't know. All I know is that I'm sitting in Vi's favorite chair, and it smells like her, which I love, and I'm just checking shit on my phone not really doing anything when she comes in with a slight frown on her face, and I think something's wrong.

"What's up, babe?" I'm not checking my phone anymore. Instead, I'm watching her fidget with that gorgeous, red, curly hair of hers as she tries to look less nervous than she actually feels.

She holds up her phone as if presenting evidence in court. "My mom texted me."

"Okay?" We haven't talked too much about family, usually because I avoid the topic, but I know she has a good relationship with her parents but doesn't see them often.

"Remember when I told you they were about to celebrate their thirtieth wedding anniversary?"

I don't but I nod anyways because I probably should. I'm not an idiot.

"Well, they've decided to have a renewing of the vows, and they want me there. Us there."

I'm about to say 'sure, no problem' until I realize two things. One, her parents live in California, so this is a weekend road trip. Together. As a couple. And two, this is not just any road trip, but a meet the parents trip.

I've never 'met the parents' for anyone. Parents usually don't want to meet the guy who bangs their little girl on occasion purely for the shared orgasms. Go figure.

But I play it cool. If I freak out, she'll freak out, and that won't be good for my cock tonight or my heart tomorrow. But if I'm too cool, she might think I'm not taking this seriously which, trust me, I am.

"What do they know about me?" I ask, buying time to figure out the best response.

She walks over, her body language more relaxed now that she sees I'm not in a state of panic. At least outwardly. When she slides onto my lap, all worry disappears into the soft curves of her sexy-as-hell body.

While my hand caresses her thigh, she fills me on the parental details. "They know we're dating. That it's getting kind of...serious?"

She says this like a question, and I know we need to talk about where this is going. We have, a bit, but there's a lot up in the air. "It is...serious," I say. "And whether I leave for tour or not, that doesn't change what I feel right now. Though, I don't know entirely how to define those feelings yet." We aren't ready for the 'L' word. At least I'm not. But it's close. "But I know I care deeply for you, Vi. And I'm not ready to walk away from you. Or us."

She rubs herself against my cock and wraps her arms around my neck. "Long distance would be hard," she says, a seductive smile on her lips.

"So hard," I say as my cock pokes against her. "I'd miss this," I say, kissing her deeply. And, God, would I ever.

There are a lot of reasons to stay in Vegas. I want to start my new life. I don't want to be on the road for another year of strip dancing. I don't want to leave Vi. I don't want to uproot myself again.

I also don't want to let the kids down. They need this after-school program. And I need the money to make that happen.

But as Vi runs her hands down my chest and pulls off my shirt, thoughts of the kids and the center and dancing float away. I want her. That's all I know.

"Will you go with me?" she asks.

It takes a moment to remember what she's talking about. Her parents. Right. "Yes. Sure, babe."

She could ask anything right now, and with her body pressed against mine with the promise of more, the answer would always be yes.

NINETEEN

Vi

It should only take about four hours to get from Las Vegas to my parents' house in Belmont Shore, California—the hip, fun part of Long Beach, where's there's actual beach.

Of course it never only takes four hours. There's always stop-and-go parking lot traffic getting in and out of Las Vegas. Which is why I try not to ever leave my beloved city. It's practically designed to make you want to stay.

But my parents are renewing their vows, and it's been too long since I've seen them outside of Skype. And they want to meet my boyfriend.

And I kinda want them to meet my boyfriend. I'm curious what they will think of Lachlan. They've met other guys I've dated. They know my kinks and my lifestyle and they've always been cool with it. I'm guessing they will be shocked to discover I'm not with a sub this time around.

I know *I* am.

We toss a coin to decide which car we should take and who gets to drive. Lachlan believes my beloved Camaro isn't safe—or big enough for his 6' 2" frame. I think his brand-new black Beemer is pretentious and boring.

So we flip. Heads the Camaro. Tails the BMW.

Heads.

I win!

The Camaro it is. And I get to drive.

We leave early, our weekend bags thrown into the trunk and *venti* cups of caffeine steaming between us. "All set?" I ask.

He nods, tucking his legs in and dramatically sighing. "I suppose. Though I might not be able to walk straight after this."

"I'll find some way of stretching you out again."

He laughs, and I rev the engine and pull out of our parking spot.

I love driving. I know not everyone does, but to me it's liberating. The road can take you anywhere, in any direction. All you need is a car and enough money for gas and the entire country is your playground.

What I don't love is bumper to bumper traffic, which is what we hit as soon as we 'park' on the 15 heading out of Vegas.

I'm half foot on the break, half ready to put pedal to the metal as soon as everyone gets out of the way. "I wonder if there's an accident."

Lachlan rolls down the window and peeks his head out. "Don't see anything. Just cars. Everywhere, cars."

"Fantastic. What shall we do to pass the time?" He winks suggestively, and I laugh. "Um, no. We might eventually have to move forward an inch, and then where would we be?"

"Happy. We'd be in Happyland while the rest of these schmucks complained and tweeted about their roadside misery of bumper to bumper madness."

"Happyland? Is this a thing now, because I'm not sure how I feel about that."

His hand lands on my thigh, riding higher and higher until his fingers graze my panties. "I can make you feel very… happy…about our Happyland. I promise."

I let go of the steering wheel and push his hand back to my knee, not without some level of regret—but still, safety first and all that shit, right? "Happyland it is. But it'll have to wait until we get to Long Beach."

"That would require movement on this freeway," he says, squeezing my knee.

"True."

"I have an idea." He pulls his hand off my knee and rummages through my glove box.

"What are you looking for?"

"Pen and paper?"

He pulls out receipts, business cards, napkins…not all of them clean. I laugh at the look on his face. And a stack of papers. "What the hell, Vi. Do you never clean this out? This has got to be your registration for the last…six years."

"What can I say? There's always something more interesting to do than clean out my car. Be glad there's no food in there."

He sticks his hand in and pulls out a half-eaten hamburger I don't remember buying. "You were saying?"

"Oh. Well, hey, I didn't tell you to go poking around in there. You entered at your own risk and without authorization. We frown on that sort of thing here in the States."

"I'll remember that." He continues to rummage until he finds what he's looking for. "Eureka! We've found gold. Well, a gold pen at any rate."

He scribbles something on the back of an old registration and then folds it. "I've written something on this paper. If you guess what it is in twenty questions, you win. If you don't, I win."

"What do we win?"

He ponders that for a moment. "Loser gives the winner a full body massage with oils."

"Agreed," I say. I could definitely think of worse ways to spend an hour than with Lach's hands all over my oily body, rubbing my muscles until I moan. Just the thought starts to make me wet.

"Okay, go!" he says. "First question."

"Can I do multiple choice?" I ask.

"Nope. Yes or no, only. Second question."

"Hey wait, that didn't count."

"Okay fine, but that's your only freebie. Now go!"

"Is it an animal?"

"No," he says.

"Inanimate object?"

"No."

"Place?"

"Yes."

"A place we've been together?"

"Not yet."

Hmm...not yet? Where could that be?

"Sixteen questions left, babe."

"Domestic?"

"It can be."

What the hell does *that* mean? "Is it someplace you've been?"

"No."

So, not Australia.

I'm having so much fun with Lachlan that I barely notice when traffic finally picks up and we're moving again. I space my questions out carefully, talking about other things in between as I consider my clues.

We're a few hours outside of Las Vegas when I have one question left, and I think I know the answer, but I'm not sure. And then the steering wheel jerks in my hand, and I nearly drive the car into the ditch on the side of the road. "What the fuck?"

I slow down and pull over, narrowly avoiding an accident with the side railing. Once parked, we get out to assess the damage. A blown left front tire.

"Ah man, that was my favorite tire," I say, kicking it.

Lachlan laughs. "You have a favorite tire on your car?"

"Yes, doesn't everyone?"

He just shakes his head and pops my trunk. "You got a spare in here?"

"Of course," I say. "I even know how to change it myself."

"I like a girl who can take care of herself." He looks me up and down, drawing my attention to my high heels, short skirt and silk blouse. "But are you sure you want to change it in that outfit? Because I'm happy to do it."

I prop a hand on my hip and consider my options. Play the damsel in distress and let my boyfriend change the tire, or ruin my outfit proving I can handle it all myself. This is actually a hard choice for me. I don't like depending on anyone else for things. It's why I learned how to change and check my oil, change my tire and assess minor engine repairs. I know a lot about this car, and while I'm not a mechanic, I know enough to not be scammed by one. But relationships can't survive with one person trying to be everything all the time—not to mention, neither would this outfit. I'm learning that with Lachlan. Sometimes we have to soften, to allow our partner to step in and lead, help, support. So I do that, and my favorite red heels thank me as Lach pulls out the tire and gets to work.

My phone bings, and I slide into the passenger seat and check it. It's a text from Zoe and it's not good.

He's being such a douchebag, I can't even. What do I do? Help!

What's he done this time? I type back, groaning inwardly.

He insists we can't have sex until we get married. He says his priest had a long talk with him and that I'm to blame for his unhappiness because I'm forcing him to live in sin by not marrying him.

"Everything okay?" Lachlan asks from the front of the car.

"Man trouble," I say through the open door.

"Zoe's guy again?"

"Who else?" Lachlan had heard enough of our conversations to know all about Zoe and her emotionally-stunted lover.

"What's he done this time?" he asks.

I fill him in and he makes a noise that is not very pleasant. "Tell her that if this guy can't take responsibility for his own choices, he's not a real man and doesn't deserve her."

I text her Lachlan's advice and wait. Her response makes me laugh.

That man of yours, does he have a brother?

LOL No. But we can definitely find you something better than this guy. Ask yourself, do you want to live with someone who blames you for his alleged sins instead of taking responsibility himself?

There's a long pause before she replies.

No. It makes me feel like shit. Like I'm a horrible person.

I look outside at Lachlan as he pulls the old tire off and sticks the spare tire on. I never feel like shit with him. He always makes me feel special, cared for, considered. Zoe deserves this. She deserves the best out there. I've kept my silence for months now, knowing it's her decision, but I can't hold my tongue any longer.

Dump him. He doesn't deserve you. And he'll never change.

Her response comes fast.

People can change.

"She says people can change," I tell Lach.

"Nope. I mean, sure, they can. But how long has she been with this guy?"

"A few years."

"And has he changed?"

"No."

"There you have it."

I text these questions to Zoe and she replies with a sad face crying emoticon.

We're yelling at each other now. I told him he's had plenty of time to figure his shit out and I'm done waiting for him to grow up. He said this would all be fixed if I'd marry him.

I shake my head and relay the new info to Lachlan.

He sighs. "The only thing marrying him would accomplish is putting her in a more permanent set of miserable circumstances."

I text that to her with my own thoughts.

His neurosis, his showers after sex, his chronic Catholic guilt taken to extremes, his blaming of you for his own shit, none of that will change by putting a ring on your finger. You have to decide if you want to be with this man BASED ON WHO HE IS RIGHT NOW. Do you want this man in front of you? AS HE IS.

Long pause. I wait nervously for her reply. Have I pushed too far? Is she freaking out? I wish I was there and could see her face to face and talk through this. But she's a grown woman, and I know she's strong enough to face this.

No. I don't want this. I'm done.

She doesn't text again for another several minutes, and Lachlan is joining me at the car, having just finished putting away the trashed tire and tools, when her next text comes.

It's done. I've kicked him out and invited Ben & Jerry to come spend the weekend with me. What have I done?

You've opened yourself to something truly great. You've freed yourself from a toxic relationship that was hurting you. Call Tate. He's great with breakups, and he'll bring Ben & Jerry's best friend Jack Daniels. You can all party together.

Great idea. Calling now. Sorry to interrupt your trip. Have fun with the parents.

You aren't interrupting anything. Hang in there, kid. You'll get through this and be stronger for it.

I put the phone down and look up at Lachlan, who's standing by the door looking so fucking sexy, and I realize we're sort of in the middle of nowhere and there's no one else around and this man is a god with his body and I'm a seriously lucky woman. "About that car sex…"

After the mind-blowing part, I pull up my panties and he tosses the condom and we would probably smoke a cigarette if we were living in an 80s television series. He holds me on his lap in the front seat and smiles. "You guessed the 20 questions."

"What?" I stroke his face, still lost in our lovemaking.

"Happyland," he says, his grin spreading. "That was the answer." He squeezes my ass. "This was the answer."

"But you said it's someplace you hadn't been," I object. Because we've clearly been here before. Many, many times.

He shakes his head. "Not in a car. That was the point. Happyland in the car. With you."

I laugh with him and kiss him again, because damn this man is amazing.

TWENTY

Lach

I've never met a girl's parents before. I expect a stubborn father who is determined I'm not good enough for his girl and a perfectionist mother who needs every detail of my life. I know I'm stereotyping.

It doesn't go as I expect.

When I knock on the door a woman yells, "Come in!" We do. The hallway is white, and a modern painting of a blue sphere hangs on the wall. Vi told me her mother's a painter. I wonder if this is one of her pieces.

Someone giggles.

A petite woman in khaki shorts and a tank top is playing Twister on the living room floor. Tangled with her limbs is a man, his arms thick, his orange shirt half unbuttoned. Two glasses of wine stand half full on the side. They notice us and wave. "Hi, honey. Just give us a second." The woman tries to move her foot to a red circle. She slips and falls and laughs. The man wraps his arm around her. They stand.

Vi gives each of them a hug. "So good to see you!" She motions at me. "This is Lachlan. Lach, these are my parents. Angela and Marvin."

I offer a handshake, but both of them embrace me instead. Angela smiles at her daughter. "He's tall."

Marvin, who reaches only my shoulder, shrugs. A streak of gray runs the side of his black hair. "Height's not that important."

Angela kisses his cheek. She has freckles and a dimple. Her hair is red. "It's okay, baby. I still love you." And then, to me, "Forgive him, he's drunk." Her face scrunches up, and she burps. "Sorry. We're both drunk."

Vi shakes her head.

I should say something witty, but nothing comes to mind. Alcohol should help. "Any more of that wine?"

Angela grabs a leopard purse off a hanger. "Not for you. You're driving."

Vi frowns. "I thought we were staying in for dinner."

"We were, until you told me Lachlan's a dancer, so…"

"So, we decided to go to a club," finishes Marvin, throwing on a leather jacket. I notice a tribal tattoo around his wrist.

"Nice tat," I say. When I imagined Vi's parents, I imagined an old couple that spends their days on the sofa, yelling at each other to pass the remote and ordering cheap takeout food for dinner. But Marvin and Angela seem like…well, they seem like Vi and me. They seem fun.

"Thanks," says Marvin. "Got it a year ago with my brother. How about you? Any tattoos?"

"Yeah, actually—"

"Okay, boys," says Angela. "You can compare tattoos later. Right now, Mama needs to party." She opens the door and Marvin follows her out.

Vi has a hand on her face, her cheeks red. "So, that's my parents."

I wrap my arms around her waist. "I like them. It's me I'm worried about."

"Just do some fancy dance moves. They'll love you."

"I hope so." I turn to go.

She grabs my hand. "You're really nervous about this, aren't you?"

"A bit."

"Really? Just a bit? Then why is your hand sweating?"

I pull my hand away and wipe it on my jeans. "Okay. A lot. I never impressed my parents."

"Your parents were assholes."

"And yours aren't."

She raises her eyebrow. "I see. So you really want to impress them. Okay. Here's the game plan." She takes my arm and walks with me outside. "For my mom, impress her with your dance moves. Also, if you could do something extremely physical, like maybe pushups while I'm sitting on you, that would help."

"Really?"

She grins. "Okay, fine. The pushups would mostly be for me." We pause outside the car. "For my dad, just talk about mixed martial arts fighting—you know, MMA. He loves it."

I grit my teeth. "I don't know anything about MMA."

She shrugs. "Then just buy him cocktails and listen. It works for me."

"Thanks."

She presses her lips to mine. "You'll do great."

We pull apart and get in the car. "Where to?" I ask.

Angela gives me the directions to a nearby club. It takes ten minutes to get there. On the way, Angela and Marvin ask me about my hobbies—working out—my favorite TV show—*Breaking Bad*—and my opinion on zoos—don't have one.

"Zoos are evil," says Angela.

"Some help educate kids," says Marvin. Vi told me he teaches theater as well as produces plays.

They keep debating as we arrive at the club. The bouncer recognizes Angela and Marvin and lets us through. Inside, tables and chairs glow lime green. People dance to a fast beat and a live DJ. Marvin grabs Angela's hand and pulls her into the crowd. Vi wraps her arms around my shoulders, and we start swaying side to side. I want to do more than dance.

Vi runs a hand down my chest. "You should show off your moves."

I'm used to performing on stage. Performing in a crowd is different. There's no choreography. I'm in control. I decide when the show starts, when it stops. Freedom is mine.

"Soon," I say.

I wait for the next song. A slow deep beat comes on. I grin and pull away from Vi, finding some space. I start simple, my body flowing with music. Some people stop to watch. A circle starts to form around me. I have more space. My legs glide over the floor, my arms forming shapes in the air, starting and stopping to the beat. The circle of people grows again. Angela and Marvin are among them, cheering. I must have a quarter of the dance floor to myself. I add spins and flips to my routine. I lock my hands behind my back and flip forward, letting my head touch the floor. It's a tricky move. Painful when done poorly. Dangerous when done wrong. I perform it perfectly. Again and again.

The crowd roars with excitement. On my final flip, I stick my arms out, and instead of landing on my feet, land straight on my back. My arms and legs help absorb the shock. It barely hurts. People gasp. This is a move few can imagine doing.

I perform a kick-up, jumping back on my feet. The bridge of the song comes on. It's faster, and so am I, isolating parts of my body as they move to the music. As the song reaches the final chorus, I begin a series of trick jumps, twisting sideways through the air. On the final note, I land a double flip. I bow my head and hold my arms up. The crowd knows my performance is over, and they erupt in howls and cheers.

I walk into the circle, joining the audience, and a woman takes my place, her hips moving to the new beat. Once a performance has begun, others want it to continue. They want the energy of the applause.

Vi, Angela, and Marvin huddle around me. Angela squeals with her arms in the air. "That was amazing. Vi, honey, this one's a keeper." So mom's impressed. Check.

Marvin shakes his head up and down to the music. "Pretty good moves." Dad still needs work. Take note.

Vi's face is red. She's biting her lip. "I'll require a private performance later."

I grin. I know just the moves I'll use. The finish will be amazing.

We head over to the bar and order drinks. Marvin talks about MMA. We all nod along. "You ever practice fighting, Lachlan?"

If you don't count a few scuffles in high school, then... "No. Dancing was always my thing."

Marvin rolls his shoulders. "You should try martial arts. There are quite a few similarities between katas and choreography. Plus, you already have the flexibility. That was my biggest challenge."

Darrel taught me stretches along with my first dance moves. Each morning, I would push my body further and further until doing the splits became easy. Then I'd push more.

Angela checks her phone. "We should head home. I'll need to get up early just to get rid of my hangover."

I finish up my drink. "Vi's got an amazing hangover cure."

Angela chuckles. "Who do you think taught her the recipe?"

. . .

The next day, Angela and Vi make everyone the secret hangover cure. We're all in the kitchen. Marvin and I cringe as we down the vile concoction. Marvin trembles. "I have a love/hate relationship with this drink. You'd think I'd be used to it. Some days I think it tastes worse."

I shrug. "You can't deny the benefits."

He nods, and we clink glasses. Angela and Vi sip their drinks, smiling and chatting the whole time. Marvin nudges my shoulder and whispers. "Sometimes, I think they've figured out how to make the damned thing taste good. They just give us the old version for fun."

I raise an eyebrow. "Or maybe they just give us a special ingredient."

He rubs his chin, frowning. "There's no way to know."

I have an idea. "Hey, babe."

Vi flips her red hair out of her face. Her grin is devilish. "What's up? Enjoying your drink?"

I rub my belly. "Oh, I loved it. In fact, I loved it so much I'm all finished. Can I have some of yours?"

She turns away, doing something on the counter. "I'll make you a second one."

"Come on. Just a sip."

"Well..." She turns back, holds out her glass. "Well, okay."

I grab it and drink. My throat burns. My eyes leak. "Oh fuck. This is like ten times worse." I run to the sink, turn on the cold water, and splash it over my tongue.

I hear Marvin's shocked voice. "What are you drinking ladies?"

The ladies giggle. "Vi added pepper when you weren't looking," says Angela.

Vi makes a clicking noise. "How's that for your special ingredient?"

I lick at the sink water. This makes no sense. "I like spicy foods. What kind of pepper is this?

"Carolina Reaper," says Vi. "Hottest pepper in the world."

My mouth cools off. I turn off the water and dry my face. Marvin pats me on the back, a sympathetic frown on his face. "Sorry, son. But I've tried as well. Like I said. There's no way to know."

Some warning would have been appreciated. But then I realize he called me *son*. I feel warmth in my belly. It might be happiness.

It might be the pepper.

I pour myself a cold glass of milk and silently swear vengeance on my girlfriend and her mother.

Marvin pulls a silver box from a closet. "Ready for the barbecue?"

"Yeah. Watch the seasonings, or we might end up with Carolina Reaper steak."

Vi pouts her lips. "I'm sorry, baby."

"No, you're not."

She caresses my face. "I am if I hurt your feelings."

I smile. "You didn't."

She steps back and her devilish grin returns. "Oh, good. Watching you lick the tap water was hilarious."

. . .

I flip the steaks over and apply a layer of barbecue sauce with a brush. Angela and Vi sit at an outdoor table overlooking a backyard of colored rocks and vibrant bushes. The landscape requires less maintenance than a field of grass and looks more beautiful. I'll have to get something similar for my house.

Marvin slides open the back door, joining us outside. "We're out of beer. I'll go grab some."

Vi taps the table. "Oh, you should take Lachlan with you."

"Great. Let's go."

I close the barbecue lid. "Sure, but the meat's not done."

Vi walks up beside me and grabs my spatula. "I'll take care of it."

I remember she doesn't like to cook. "You sure?"

"Of course."

I slip off my barbecue glove and pass it to her. "Thank you." I kiss her on the lips. It's hard to pull away.

I walk into the house. Marvin and I throw on our jackets. We're halfway out the door when we hear the scream. I rush back outside.

Vi is cradling her hand. "It burned me!"

"Let me see." I examine her. There's a small red spot on her index finger. It will heal easily. "You're fine. What happened?"

She sways her arms. "I...um...tried to flip the meat."

"With your hand?"

She huffs and looks indignant. It's adorable. "No. Of course not. I flipped it with the spatula, just, right off the grill. Then I tried to lift the steak. It hurt."

I notice the piece of meat on the wooden patio. I chuckle and hug Vi. "Does this make it better?"

"A little. Thank you so much—oh shit!" She spins toward the grill, turns off the heat, and opens it. The meat is black. "Shit. I burned it." She bites her lip. I can see she's close to crying.

I laugh to diffuse the tension. "What are you talking about? The crispy bits are my favorite. It's Cajun style."

Vi smiles as I begin to serve the food.

Angela takes a bite and looks at Marvin. "She still cooks better than you."

...

We finish what we can of the steak, and Vi offers to show me around town. She wants to show me where she grew up. I can't say no.

She drives me to her old high school, where her favorite teacher taught art, and to the mall, where she hung out with friends. She drives to the movie theater she used to frequent, and we watch a romantic comedy. She drives to the restaurant she loved, and we eat a pair of burgers. She drives to the beach.

We sit on the sand and watch the sun set, and I toss rocks into the ocean. "Is this where you brought all your boyfriends?" I ask, jokingly.

Instead of laughing, Vi frowns. "One. Pete. He was kind of like you."

"No one's like me."

She rolls her eyes. "No, of course not. I just mean, he wasn't a sub. All my friends had a crush on him."

Not all guys can handle talking about exes. I don't mind. It lets me learn more about Vi. I can tell this guy affected her. "Not that I'm complaining, but what happened?"

She tosses a stone into the water. "I crashed my car. I had a black eye the size of a pinecone." She sounds casual. The crash must have been minor. "The next week, we all went to an amusement park. I couldn't go on most of the rides. Pete could. That weekend, I caught him and my best friend making out in his car."

I wrap my arm around her. I'm starting to see why she had trouble with me taking control. "That's horrible. And stupid. What kind of guy chooses a roller coaster over you?"

"I know. Fucking bastard."

"And with your friend…"

"Yep. She's the reason I have a hard time with female friends. And you'd think that because I know that, it'd be easier, but it's not." Vi tosses another stone. It falls with a big wet thud.

She leans against my shoulder. "I'm glad I found you."

I kiss the top of her head. "For the record, if you can't ride a roller coaster, you can always ride me."

TWENTY ONE

Vi

I do ride him. On my double bed in my old room with Patrick Swayze staring at us from his *Dirty Dancing* poster still hanging on my wall. What can I say? I guess I've always had a thing for dancers.

We try to be quiet. And fail. The bed squeaks as I rise and fall on his cock. And I can't help but giggle and lean over, my breasts brushing against his mouth as we balance between erotic and comical. I feel like I'm in high school again, and any minute my parents will come in and send my boyfriend packing. They're liberal, but not *that* liberal. At least not when their daughter was sixteen.

When my giggles get the best of me, Lach flips me over with an expert move and uses his whole body to make me forget about parents or my red comforter or my old journal still stuck between the bars under my bed. All of those thoughts disappear as he makes love to me, holding me, caressing me, making my body feel every touch, every sensation, every shudder of pleasure.

It feels like we just fell asleep when the sound of my mother singing downstairs wakes us up.

Lach rolls to face me, his eyes slits in his handsome face as he tries to focus through the haze of sleep. "What is that?"

"Country music," I say. "My mom must be making pancakes. She always sings country when making pancakes."

"I will pay her a million dollars to stop and let us sleep for just a few more hours."

Snuggling closer to him under the covers, our naked bodies fitting so nicely together, I don't entirely disagree…but… "We have to get up. You can't come all the way to Belmont Shores and not have her pancakes. She makes the best pancakes the world has ever known."

"So you didn't get your cooking skills from your mother, I take it." He's smiling, and I smack his arm.

"Shush, you," I say with mock ferocity, though I'm smiling too. "I have other skills. Now get moving."

He pulls me back into his arms as I try to escape the bed. "Oh, I'm fully acquainted with those skills. In fact…" his hands dip between my legs and rub against my clit, "I think we should explore those skills more fully in the light of day. If 6am can rightfully be called *day*."

It's hard. So very hard. But I pull away and stand, shrugging into clothes before he can lure me back into the den of temptation and warmth. "Nice try, lover boy. But you'll soon thank me for dragging your tired ass out of bed."

He follows me begrudgingly downstairs, and the smell of fried batter and cinnamon and sugar greet us. My mom hands us each a cup of coffee and points Lachlan to the cream and sugar. "Didn't know how you like it, so feel free to spice it up. Breakfast will be ready soon."

She flips a pancake in her pan and starts up again with another country song. I sigh and smile and sip my coffee. She remembers how I like it. Being home is strange, in a wonderful kind of way. I have so many memories of this place, but they all seem so long ago. Everything feels smaller, and I know it's not just the size, because honestly I'm not really any bigger than I was in high school. It's the scope. The world has opened up before me and the possibilities are now mine to create. This home sheltered me, gave me a safe haven, a nest to grow in. But then I left and everything felt scarier, bigger, more dangerous. But also more exciting.

Still, it's nice to be back and visit your safety nest once in a while. To remember that you're not alone and someone has your back somewhere. My parents are always that for me.

I glance at Lachlan, who's staring at me as he drinks his coffee. I wonder what he's thinking. If he's comparing our childhoods. Our families. Our lives. He doesn't have that safety nest. That feel-good memory of home and hearth. That place to go back to when life gets a little too big. My heart cracks a little for him, and I hope that on some level he can adopt my family, my home, to be a safe place for him.

My mom serves us both and calls my dad in, who was out in the garden pulling weeds. I wait and watch Lachlan take his first bite.

And I smile as he has his first foodgasm. Trust me, it's a thing.

After rolling his eyes back and smiling and groaning and moaning, he finally swallows.

"What did I tell you?" I ask.

"You were right. I will never question you again, my Queen. Angela, these are the best anything I've ever tasted in my life."

My mom smiles and pats his hand. "They're yours any-time you want to come over."

"It's not that long a drive from Vegas," he announces as he devours his plate. "We could probably make this a weekly thing. What do you say, Vi?"

I just laugh and keep eating. My mom has this effect on people. It's a miracle I ever moved out.

. . .

We spend the rest of the day walking around Belmont Shores, exploring the shops, eating lunch at BJ's Pizza—which, to Lachlan's dismay, doesn't actually serve blow jobs—and enjoying the shoreline.

That night, we get ready for something my parents planned for the four of us, a mystery cruise dinner. The premise is simple. We board a ship for a few hours while a cast of actors perform a murder mystery that we have to solve while eating dinner and dessert.

Easy enough.

When we arrive we are nearly late because as lovable as my parents are, timely and prompt they are not. I have to whisper sweet nothings into Lachlan's ear to calm him. Apparently he's the 'prompt' type and gets really stressed at the thought of being late. He's convinced the ship has left without us when we arrive five minutes late, but we have plenty of time and board in high spirits.

Before we enter, we are given the opportunity to take pictures together holding various weapons. Lachlan laughs and picks up a wicked looking plastic knife. "The dancer, in the bedroom, with a knife," he says.

"You are ridiculous," I say, smiling.

He nuzzles my neck. "You won't be saying that when I sheathe my big knife into you later," he says.

I slap him away, laughing and pick up a gun. "This looks good on me."

He pulls me into a kiss. "Everything looks good on you, babe."

The photographer grabs a few shots and then takes pictures of my parents, who make out worse than us. I'd tell them to get a room, but they probably would. And really, who am I to talk at this point?

When we see the bar in the corner with a bartender ready to pour, everyone smiles. "Drinks are on me," Lachlan says. Oh, boy.

I take the liberty of ordering for everyone while my parents get our seats at one of the round tables in the back. When the bartender gives me a confused look, I take him through the mixed drinks I know my parents like best.

We've already burned a hole in Lachlan's pocket by the time the show starts, and the heat of the alcohol is making my body fuzzy and happy.

It's hard to focus on the show. Someone dies. Some other people are talking. I have to pee.

I make my way—carefully and a bit wobbly in my red high heels—down the stairs and to the tiny bathroom. After I'm done, I'm about to leave when Lachlan suddenly appears, blocks my exit and pushes me back in with his body. He closes the door behind him and rubs his hands over my back as he nibbles my neck. "You are fucking gorgeous," he says.

I can taste rum on his mouth as he kisses me. "What are you doing here?" I ask. "You're missing the show."

"I already know the killer," he says.

"You do?" This surprises me. I'm not even sure I know who the victim is, let alone the killer.

"Yes, it's the cousin who owned the dry cleaner. They did it for the money and revenge. The email addresses gave it away."

I nod, totally lost but willing to believe him because his hand just slid up my skirt and I don't care about fake murders or emails, I just want this sexy, delicious man standing in front of me.

He hikes up my skirt, pulls aside my panties and spreads me, then lifts me onto his hips, holding me up by my ass as he uses the walls of the bathroom to brace me.

When he enters me, everything crystallizes into just me and him. Nothing else exists. He fills me and makes a fire burn deep in my belly as he pushes his hips into mine, entering me deeper and deeper, his fingers digging into my flesh, deliciously tight and so fucking hot.

This position stimulates my clit and my nipples as every part of our body connects, and when I come it's hard and deep and it sends him over the edge pretty fucking fast.

When we go back upstairs, I feel confident we've covered our tracks. I put myself back together and fix my hair and clothes and no one knows, right?

We eat some cake and fill out some forms (I copy Lachlan's answers, because I, obviously, don't know shit about what happened) and then my parents disappear for a tad too long.

When they come back, I'm horrified.

My mom has a big smile on her face, and my dad looks like the cat that ate the canary. If the canary was my mom. Yuck.

"You kids sure know how to pick 'em," he says. "That bathroom was just the trick."

I feign gagging sounds. "I can't believe we've had sex in the same place as my parents."

My mom laughs. "Oh, honey, you're so funny. You think we've never gotten it on in your bedroom?"

My face turns red, and Lachlan laughs with them while I die a slow and painful death. Thank God there's more alcohol.

TWENTY TWO

Lach

We all regret the liberal use of the bar the night before, but we recover with some help from Vi and her mother and spend a relaxed day getting ready for the renewal ceremony taking place at sunset on the beach.

Most everything has already been set up, from catering to flowers, and it's a pretty casual affair. I'm not sure what I was expecting this weekend. I knew I'd be meeting Vi's parents. And I guess some part of my brain knew that it wouldn't be just the four of us at her parent's renewal ceremony. Honestly, I just didn't give it that much thought. Which is why I'm a bit shell-shocked at having to meet and socialize with the entire Reynolds clan. Because, from what I can tell, every single fucking member of her family and extended family has come for this, from the youngest babies to the oldest grandparents. And they all want to meet Vi's new boyfriend. Good thing I'm used to putting on a game face.

We walk to the beach from Angela and Marvin's home. It's just down the street, and they greet their neighbors as they walk by, Marvin in khakis and a Grateful Dead t-shirt, Angela in a white satin sundress. No one wears shoes. Vi looks drop-dead fuckable in an emerald green sundress that rides her thighs, and suddenly I want to be back in her bedroom under those sheets instead of trudging through sand to where floral arrangements and white wooden chairs await.

It's hard to find a bad weather day in Southern California, and today is no exception. It's fall, so the beaches aren't as crowded as I imagine they would be in summer, but the sun is shining, light glinting off the waves.

It reminds me of Australia a little. The perpetual summer and wide expanses of beaches. I spent a lot of time by the shore as a kid growing up with no one to go home to. Being near the ocean again, even if it's not the right ocean, settles something in me I didn't know was unsettled.

I take a deep breath and smile as Vi holds my hand and introduces me to aunts, uncles, her mother's parents who look tanned and active and happy to be here, and too many cousins running around to count. There are children, teens, tweens and adults in all stages of life gathered here in various states of dress from crazy casual to over-the-top formal. No one seems to care what anyone else is wearing or not wearing. Everyone is smiling, laughing, hugging and finding seats before the ceremony begins.

"I've got to go help my mom get ready," Vi says, squeezing my hand. "Will you be okay on your own for a bit?"

It's sweet that she asks, and I nod. "I'm good. You go ahead." I kiss her forehead and she leans into it, exhaling as my lips touch her skin. This woman. She's undoing me in the best way possible.

I watch as she walks away and don't notice Marvin until he's standing next to me fiddling with a bow tie. Over his Grateful Dead t-shirt.

"She's something special, isn't she?" he asks, watching his daughter.

"She is," I agree, a smile creeping onto my face.

Marvin turns to me. "I've never seen her this happy. Don't break my little girl's heart."

"It's the last thing I want to do," I tell him, and I mean it. The thought of hurting Vi crushes me.

"You know, son, Vi told us the sticky spot you're in with your dreams to open a youth program and the pressure to tour for another year."

My heart thumps a bit harder in my chest when he calls me son. It's stupid, I know. An adolescent fantasy that was never fulfilled. But somehow, it feels good. Even if it does make me feel ten years old. "Yes," I say, wondering where this conversation is going.

"Have you considered trusting the Universe on this?" he asks in all seriousness.

I can hear the capitalization of 'Universe' in his voice and prepare myself for a hippy, new age conversation on existentialism or some shit. Don't get me wrong, I don't think believing this stuff is bad, it's just never been my path. I'm not sure what my path is, but I know it doesn't involve crossing my fingers and hoping some outside force will fix my problems. "It's been my experience that hard work and determination get you further than trust," I tell him, hoping I'm not loosing cool 'son' points with my honesty.

He nods, his expression thoughtful. "I appreciate that. And I admire a person who works hard and carves his own path in life. But what I mean is, have you considered that you've maybe overthought this? That in planning down to the detail, you've erased any opportunity for magic to happen?" He holds up a hand before I can protest. "I know what you're going to say. I can see the skepticism in your eyes. Just hear me out. Try holding the intention of what you want in your heart of hearts and seeing if the details don't rearrange themselves to give you what you need—what you want—even if it's not what you think it should look like. That's all I'm saying. Sometimes, we think we know exactly what we *want*, but when we open ourselves up to the unexpected, we get what we *needed* all along."

I look at Vi again. She isn't the kind of girl I would have thought I'd be with. Hell, I never thought I'd be with anyone for more than a few nights. But she's perfect for me in every way. I consider Marvin's words and wonder how they might apply to my problem with the after-school center. Could I be holding on to a vision that's keeping me from making the true magic of my ideas work? I don't know.

Marvin pats me on the back. "Good man. I can see you're at least thinking about it." He pulls off his bow tie and hands it to me. "Get rid of this thing for me, will ya? Who wears a bow tie with a t-shirt anyways? And while you're at it, would you mind standing in as my witness? My wife already snagged our daughter, so it looks like I'm in need of someone on my side."

. . .

As we stand there, waiting for Vi and Angela to walk down the makeshift aisle of white and pink rose petals, for a moment I feel displaced. This could be me and Vi someday. Music starts and I see her first, walking slowly toward me in a vision of green with that wild red hair and my heart swells. The thought of us standing here in front of friends and family doesn't scare me like it would have before. I wink at her, and she grins and takes her place at the front.

Our eyes rarely stray from each other's through the service, and I wonder if she's thinking the same thing. That someday we'll be here, celebrating our love. And maybe after twenty-five years, this will also be us, with kids and family and a lifetime of memories and still having sex in bathrooms and making each other laugh.

The ceremony is fast, back-dropped by a sunset to rival all. As the sky glows in oranges and reds and yellows, we snack on the buffet provided and drink liberally and crowd around to watch Marvin and Angela open their gifts.

When Angela pulls a purple gift bag from the pile, Vi nudges me. "This one's from us."

"Us?"

She links arms with me and leans her head against my shoulder. "Yep. I put your name on it."

I watch and wonder what "we" got her parents for their anniversary. Angela pulls a box out of the bag and laughs. "Oh my!" She holds it up for everyone to see and some of the older adults gasp. "Thank you, Vi and Lachlan. I'm sure we'll put this bondage kit to good use tonight."

Well, that's decided. We're obviously driving home today, because no way do either of us need to hear that tonight. Vi grins at me as if she can read my mind. Saucy vixen probably can.

"There's one more thing in there," she says.

I think it can't get worse.

It does.

Her mother holds up a giant purple dildo and raises an eyebrow. Marvin grabs it and slaps his leg. "Well isn't this something. A chew toy. Now we need to get a dog, Ang."

I take another drink.

TWENTY THREE

Vi

The store has been busy today. So busy that Zoe and I have had very little time to chat and catch up since I got back from my weekend home with Lach. I can tell she spent time crying and drinking, which I don't blame her for a bit. Even though the guy was a complete Douche (with a capital *D*, of course), he was in her life for a long time, and it's hard to make that kind of change, even if it's for the best. So I've been covering the floor while she stays mostly in the back doing inventory. But now we're locking up, turning off the lights and getting ready to hang out with Kacie, Tate and Sebastian, when she turns to me with a small frown.

"I think I need to pass on tonight. I'm not up for hanging out."

"Zoe, what's going on? You've been off all day, and I know it's more than just the breakup." She averts her eyes, and I can tell it's something big. "Zoe? Spill it, girl. No judgment from me, I swear."

She sighs and leans against the glass of our front door. "You know that night you said to call Tate to cheer me up?"

Uh-oh. "Yeah?"

"Well, he came over. We drank and ate junk food and watched movies, and drank some more and…"

"Oh, God. You didn't!"

Her chin drops to her head. "We did. We slept together."

My first impulse is to laugh, because while I would totally love for two of my best friends to hook up, it should not be Tate and Zoe. They wouldn't mix at all. But I can tell this is a big deal for her, so I suppress my grin and put a hand on her arm. "How do you feel about it?"

"Confused. I love Tate, but not like that. It was fun, but I'm not interested in it happening again. But what if he is? What if I've ruined our entire friendship dynamic?"

I raise an eyebrow. "You really think Tate is suddenly eager to settle down? I think you're safe on that count. Just tell him how you feel. He's probably freaking out right now thinking you want more, and he doesn't want to hurt you and fuck everything up. He'll be relieved."

A gleam of hope lights in her eyes. "Really? Because I do love him. He's the best, and I couldn't stand losing his friendship because we got carried away one lonely crazy night."

"I'm sure. Tell him how you feel. You'll both feel better for it. Do it tonight."

She straightens her back and puts on a face that looks like she's ready to go into battle. She's adorable. "Okay, I will. Thanks, Vi."

As we walk to our cars, I can't help but ask, "So, how was it? Is he any good in the sack?"

She blushes and laughs and slaps my arm before nodding. "Yeah, he's actually pretty amazing. I haven't had an orgasm that wasn't self-generated in years. It was nice."

"Glad to hear it. Maybe it's just what you needed. Someone safe and who cares about you to help you over that hump."

She sticks the key into her car and smiles. "I hadn't thought about it that way, but maybe. If he feels the same, I'll be so relieved. But don't tell Kacie, okay? I don't really want anyone else knowing."

"I won't tell her," I promise. "But Tate probably will. They tell each other everything."

Her face drops, and I smile. "Don't worry, she won't care. Come on, everything will be fine, you'll see."

. . .

When we get to our favorite bar, Tate, Kacie and Sebastian are already waiting for us. Kacie grins when she sees us walking in. "We thought you were going to bail on us."

"Nah, we just had to close up. Busy day."

"So business is going well?" Sebastian asks.

Zoe, studiously avoiding eye contact with Tate, nods. "Sure is."

"I'm glad to hear it," he says as he drops his hand on Kacie's knee. The two of them together are too cute for words. If I wasn't falling hard for my own hottie, I might gag a little.

Tate stands, and I can tell he's avoiding Zoe as well. "First round's on me," he says. "What's everyone's choice of poison?"

We put in our orders and, as he leaves to order our drinks, I nudge Zoe. "Why don't you go help him? He won't be able to carry it all."

She gives me her version of the evil eye, which comes across about as evil as a puppy trying to look fierce, and follows

Tate to the bar. I can see them talking and hope that it goes well for them both and they can get over this awkwardness.

Kacie eyes me for a moment. "Do you know?"

"I know some things. What do you know?"

"I know my brother is freaking out, and I know why," she says.

"I know why Zoe is also freaking out."

Sebastian looks at the both of us. "What am I missing?"

Kacie grins and pats his arm. "I'll tell you later."

"Are they on the same page?" I ask, hoping for Zoe's sake they are.

"If that page involves friendship and a mutually satisfying one-time experience, then yes."

I sigh in relief. I was pretty sure I was right, but getting confirmation doesn't hurt. "I'm so glad."

Sebastian looks over at Tate and Zoe and then back at us. "Oh, I see. They slept together, didn't they?"

"I'm impressed, doctor," Kacie says, snuggling up to him.

"I'm not oblivious to everything, even if I am blinded by your beauty," he says, kissing her nose.

Tate and Zoe come back with our drinks, laughing and talking like old friends. Zoe leans over and whispers *thank you* in my ear, and I pat her hand and sip my cocktail.

"I feel like we don't get together enough anymore," I say. "I miss all your faces."

Kacie nods. "Me too. Things are just crazy. The babies, work, finding time for my handsome husband. It's a lot. All wonderful and fantastic but a lot."

"I understand," I say.

I look to Tate. "What's up with you, dude?"

He glances at Zoe and back at me. "Oh, you know. The usual."

I can't ask him about women because obviously there's no one new if he just slept with Zoe, but he beats me to the punch.

"After recent events, I've realized I need a time out from women. To figure out what I want before I mess up any important relationships in my life."

I can tell even Kacie is surprised. "So you're giving men a try?" she asks teasingly.

Playing along, I grin. "It's the Aussie Posse. They converted you, didn't they? No shame in that. They converted me. At least, one of them did."

Tate laughs. "No, I'm just…on a sex fast."

"That·sounds awful," I say. "But I've been there, done that, though never deliberately."

Sebastian takes a drink from his beer. "I think it's a good move. Sometimes you need less distraction to figure things out."

Tate raises his glass to toast him. "Exactly."

Kacie looks back at me. "How are things with Lachlan? Boy can that man dance."

Sebastian gasps. "Do I need to worry, Mrs. Donovan? Perhaps I should take up dance lessons."

"You don't need to worry, but I'll never say no to seeing him dance," she says.

"Lach and I are doing great. Mostly. I mean, we have a ton of fun together. He gets along with my parents and they love him. I…I might even love him. But I don't know where we're headed. He may be leaving on another tour with his group for a year."

Tate frowns. "That seriously sucks."

"If you think you might be falling for him, maybe it's worth trying it long distance?"

I shrug. "Maybe. I don't know. I just don't like the idea of him leaving. And of not knowing one way or the other. That's the hardest part. The not knowing."

"Have you told him that?" Kacie asks.

"No," I say. "I don't want my feelings for him to affect his decisions."

"You need to tell him," Sebastian says. "Because in the end, it's his choice, but he should have all the information in order to make that choice. By not telling him, you're removing the choice from him."

I gulp down the last of my cocktail. "I hadn't thought about it like that."

Zoe nods in agreement. "A wise person once told me you should just tell him how you feel. That you'll both feel better for it."

Beaten with my own words! "You're right. You're all right. Tonight, when he gets home from work...I'll tell him."

"That you don't want him to leave?" Kacie asks.

I nod. "And...that I've fallen in love with him."

TWENTY FOUR

Lach

I'm sitting on the couch watching *Raiders of the Lost Ark* when Vi gets home from the night with her friends. I was invited but I had a show tonight and had to pass.

Vi looks nervous when she comes in, clutching her purse in her hand like she's scared of a mugger.

"What's up, babe? Did you have fun tonight?"

She nods and comes to sit next to me. "Yeah, it was fun."

I put my arm around her, expecting her to settle against my body, but she doesn't. Okay, I guess we're talking. I turn the volume down on the television and tilt my body to face her.

"I've got something to tell you, Lachlan," she says through pinched lips. "I'm not sure how you're going to react."

"Okay. I'm listening." If she's about to break up with me, shit will not end well for me. But I can't imagine that's the conversation we're about to have. I mean, shit, that would be so out of the blue. Still, I'm a bag of raw nerves as I wait for her to spit it out.

"You know how you have to decide soon about your contract and whether to renew and keep touring?"

"Yes." It's been on my mind more than ever lately.

"I don't want to tell you what to do with your own life, but I want you to know that I'd be really heartbroken if you left." She pauses, her eyes pained. "I'd rather you stayed."

I sigh in relief. "That's what you're worried about? Babe, I don't want to go either. And I'd be heartbroken, too."

She smiles, the tension in her shoulders easing a bit, but not entirely. "There's one more thing."

"Okay."

As she speaks, her words ramble together in one long sentence with no breaks or pauses or commas. "Lachlan I know you might not be ready to hear this or say it back and I don't want you to say it just because you think you should but—"

I stop her with a kiss, then I pull away, my hand cupping her head. "Vi, I love you."

Her eyes glisten with tears. "You do?"

"Yes. I've known awhile but I was waiting for the right time to tell you. I was waiting until I knew what our future would hold. But I love you, Vi. You're the most amazing woman I've ever met. I've never told anyone this before."

She smiles. "Neither have I. I love you, too."

And as Indiana Jones runs away from a giant boulder, I make love to the woman I love and we fall asleep on the couch together to old movies.

The next day I don't tell Vi my plans. She's already at work when I get up and head out.

First, I pick up groceries and drive to Kevin's. He sits on the sidewalk in front of his house, tossing a tennis ball up and down. His skateboard lies next to him. He has dark circles under his eyes. "Hey, Lach. What up?"

"Not much. Why aren't you practicing?"

He groans and smacks the board. "The wheels broke off again."

"Let me take a look." I do. The thing is beyond repair. I sit beside Kevin. "I'll get you a new one, buddy."

He rolls his eyes. "Like a year from now? No thanks." This isn't like him.

I frown. "Hey, what's going on?"

"Nothing. Just don't need your help."

"Okay. If you want, you could help me out with something in exchange."

He stands up and turns away. "I don't care about the board. You don't have to..." His shoulders droop. He sighs. "You barely come around anymore."

I've been busy, with work, with investors, with Vi, but I don't tell any of that to Kevin, because it shouldn't have gotten in the way. "I'm sorry, Kev. I'll come by more often again."

He turns back and grins. It's the way I used to grin to my parents. It's hollow. "Thanks. How's your center going?"

"It's not. I failed to get any investors."

"No way." He sits back down, puts a hand on my shoulder. "Man, there's got to be more suits out there you can talk to."

I shrug. "Sure, but—"

"But what? You got a good idea. You got the skills. Now you just need the money. It's simple."

I smirk. "Yeah. There might be a way. It might even be easier."

"Okay. Yeah, what is it?"

"I can tour again. And with the money, I won't even need an investor. I'll have full control of the center."

Kevin pulls back, shaking his head. "I don't know, man. Tour again? I thought you said you were tired of that."

"I am. I'm tired of touring. But I'm also tired of investors trying to change my vision."

"So the question is, what are you tired of more?"

"Your smart-ass wisdom," I joke. But he's got a point. There must be a right answer to my problems. Even if it's an answer I don't want to hear.

I tap him on the back and stand up. "Come on, let's see what your mom's up to."

He follows me up the porch. "Probably burning the lasagna again."

"Hey, be respectful. It's only happened like ten times." I smirk.

He smiles. There's more warmth to it now. He leads me inside the dimly lit house. The air is hazy and thick. Mary stirs a pot on the stove. She wipes her hands and adjusts her glasses. Her hair has streaks of grey. She hasn't dyed it. She must be busier than usual. "Lachlan, my boy, you remembered not to knock."

"Family doesn't knock." I slip off my shoes and hand Mary the groceries.

She examines them and sighs. "The organic chicken again? And I thought you were learning."

We all chuckle. I grab the chicken. "I'll bake it."

"No. You don't need to...ah, who am I kidding, it will go perfect with the tomato soup I'm making. Stick the thing in the oven." She eyes Kevin. "Is there something you're forgetting, Kevin McAllister?"

He groans. "My shoes." He walks back to the door and kicks them off.

I start on the chicken, seasoning it with pepper, while Mary mixes her soup and Kevin cuts up carrots. We eat dinner together. Under the table, Mary rubs her foot, gritting her teeth. She makes her holy shit face. "Stupid heels. Bill lowered my pay, so I'm working extra just to make the same."

I want to walk down the street to Bill's Burgers and punch Bill in the face, tell him to treat Mary better. I've considered it before, but Mary's asked me not to. Bill would fire her. And she's right, he would.

When I open my center, it will need employees. Mary will be the first. I turn to Kev. "How's school, man?"

He plays with his food. "Okay."

Mary drops her fork on the table. "Okay? What about that fight you got into? And that D in math?"

He crosses his arms. "I don't want to talk about it."

Mary shakes her head and turns to me. "He's not doing well, Lach. He—"

"I'm doing fine," interrupts Kevin.

"Kevin McAllister, you will not speak to me in that tone."

"Or what? What can you do? My life already sucks."

Mary stands up. "Go to your room, now."

Kevin clenches his fists. "Fine." He storms down the hallway. His door slams shut.

Mary shakes her head and sits down. There's sorrow on her face. "Sorry about that. We've been at each other's throats all week."

I grab her hand across the table. "Family can be like that. But as long as it's not like that all the time, I say it's worth it." It's more than I had.

Mary wipes her eyes. They're close to tears. "I'm glad Kevin has someone like you in his life. He's never had anyone but me. Not even his own father..." She dabs her eyes with a napkin. "I'm sorry. It's late. I...I need to rest." She cleans up her plates. "Finish your food before you leave. Goodnight, Lachlan."

"Goodnight."

With a final pained smile, she disappears into her room. I finish my food and do all the dishes, including ones already in the sink. My phone buzzes. I ignore it. I clean the counters and table. When I'm finished, I turn off the lights and head out. As I'm halfway out the door, Kevin emerges from his room.

He looks pale in the moonlight. "If you go on tour, you won't be around."

I nod. "Not for a year."

"You know, it's okay, if you need to go. I'll be fine. I won't screw up."

My chest feels lighter. "I know you won't. You're the smartest dude I know."

"Thanks, Lach."

"Get some sleep, Kev."

"I will."

We smile at each other, and I leave, knowing whatever I decide, Kevin will be fine, because he's like me. He sees the good in life.

The first part of my night is complete. For the second, I drive to the Wynn and meet Darrel at Sinatra's. He's been calling me the past few days. He needs a decision.

He shakes my hand as we are seated. "How are things with the center?"

"As they should be."

The waiter asks for our order. Darrel gets the steak. I get a small salad. I don't expect to be long.

Darrel smiles his bright smile. "I spoke to my associates, and we're willing to offer you half a million more. You will also regain your solos. Duke has done a feeble job." He holds out his hand. "So, what do you say, Lach? Will you tour with me again?"

Two-and-a-half million. The chance to perform. To entertain. My heart pounds at the opportunity. My palms sweat. "Before I answer, I have a question for you."

Darrel drops his hand, leans closer. "Yes?"

I gather my courage and ask the question I've pondered for years. "Why did you help me?"

He chuckles. It's so simple to him. "I was looking for young dancers. You had potential."

"So it was all about the money."

"Of course. Wasn't it about the money for you?"

It was a part of it. But only a small part. Entertaining people, making them happy, is what drove me. "Thank you for your answer. Now, here's my decision." I tell him. He understands.

I say goodbye and stand. As I'm about to leave, Darrel grabs my hand. "It wasn't all about the money. When we trained, you reminded me how joyful dancing could be. You reminded me of why I started. Sometimes, I wish I could go back to that again."

"Maybe we both can."

I leave with my mind clear. On the way home, I stop by a store and consider buying rum. No. I need something else tonight.

When I enter the apartment, Vi jumps off the couch. She's wearing a red shirt. Her cheeks are pale.

I close the door behind me. "I need to tell you something."

"What?" I can tell she's nervous now. Like I was last night.

I wrap my arms around her. "I said no to the tour, because I can't go. A piece of me would stay behind. You, Vi. I love you." I pull two necklaces from my pocket, a silver puzzle piece on each. "These are for us. So that no matter where we are, we remember that where we belong is together. You are my missing piece."

TWENTY FIVE

Vi

He loves me. That's the thought that keeps running through my mind. He loves me. And I love him. And we're in love. My hand strays to the silver puzzle piece on the delicate silver strand around my throat. The one that fits his. It makes me smile and feel warm and gooey inside.

I've turned into such a lovesick sap, and I couldn't be happier.

But right now I have to stay focused, because these cock rings aren't going to sell themselves.

Zoe isn't here yet. Her shift starts in a few minutes, so I'm not worried. Today I'm opening and she's closing. It's most fun when our work time overlaps, though. That's when the giggles happen.

When a college-age couple comes in looking nervous but excited, I pull myself together, put away my phone—hey, I own the shop, I can sext my boyfriend when I want—and walk over to help them.

The girl can barely make eye contact with me. She's beautiful. Dark mocha skin, big eyes, long hair. Her boyfriend looks like the college nerdy guy who always steps up to the plate. He's sweet, gentle, and holding her hand in a way that makes me like him. A lot.

"Hi there," I say with a big smile. "Welcome to Whipped. Are you looking for anything in particular?"

The girl doesn't speak, which doesn't surprise me. The guy clears his throat and proceeds, reluctantly.

"Yeah," he says. "We wanted to try experimenting with… um…anal sex. But I don't want to hurt her. So, um…" He looks down at his sneakers. "I was—we were—thinking maybe we could try some of that cream that numbs?"

"It's great that you want to try something new," I say. "We don't actually sell that cream here, and I'll tell you why. There are some serious health risks to using that."

The girl's eyes widen and the guy squeezes her hand and says, "We don't want to do anything dangerous."

I smile. "That's good. And anal sex can be safe and very pleasurable, if done correctly. Keep in mind that it can take a few weeks or months to prepare a woman for full anal penetration."

I step to the side and pull an anal plug kit from the wall. "I recommend starting with these and a good lube. Start with the smallest and go up incrementally." I look at the girl. "As you're able to take bigger sizes, you'll become more comfortable. You can also do finger play during this time, which I'd recommend. Eventually you'll be ready to try a penis. But start slow and only do what you're comfortable with. Also, many women prefer using an enema before anal play. It's often more comfortable for both parties involved."

They nod in unison and I take the anal plugs, lube, and a useful brochure on anal sex and stick it in a bag. "Is there anything else I can help you with?"

They both shake their heads. The guy pays in cash and they rush out of the store as if being chased, nearly crashing into Zoe as she comes in.

She looks at them and then at me. "Are you chasing our customers away again?" she teases.

"Ha, no. Anal sex is freaking them out. Honestly, I wish there was better education out there about healthy sexual options so people knew what they were doing without getting hurt. They wanted numbing cream."

She wrinkles her cute nose. "Hey, maybe we could start offering educational classes? It could be fun."

I nod and smile. "That's a great idea. Let's brainstorm some ideas today and see what we come up with."

She waggles her mismatched nails at me and grins. "Nope, not until you tell me what happened with you and Lach. You sounded positively giddy in your text last night. I want details!"

I show her the necklace and tell her about our *I love you*s and she squeals and dances around. "Oh-em-gee, I'm so happy for you! This is amazing! We should go out and celebrate tonight. Drinks?"

"Oh, I can't. I promised Lachlan I'd work out with him."

She grins in an expectant way, and then she frowns. "Oh, wait, you were serious?"

I place a hand on my hips. "Yes, I was serious."

She starts to laugh and I scowl at her. "What is so funny?"

"Just the thought of you..." she can't finish her sentence because she is almost out of breath, bent over our lube display in bouts of laughter. "You...working out...at an actual gym."

"Hey now, I resent that. I work out."

She wipes a tear from her eye. "Oh, really? When? When was the last time you worked out?"

I think about it and then snap my fingers. "With Kacie. I went running with Kacie!"

"Once. You went running *once* with her and it lasted about half a block. You got a cramp and swore you couldn't keep going and she had to practically carry you back."

"Who told you that?"

"You did, dork. God, I can't believe he's gotten you to agree to work out. I'm impressed. The man has skills outside the bedroom."

Okay, so maybe working out isn't my thing. Maybe I mostly keep my figure through healthy eating and good genes, but that's no reason to mock. Honestly. Some people.

She ribs me the rest of the day and I attempt to take it in stride. But as I grab my purse and my—*gulp*—gym bag, and get ready to leave, I'm suddenly nervous. What if I make an ass out of myself? Is this really the best way to kick off the 'I love you' phase of our relationship? Me next to all those hot, sexy, female gym rats who probably live to work out?

Oh God, what have I done?

. . .

When I arrive at Lach's gym, my nerves are anything but assuaged. It looks hardcore. The kind of gym you go to when you are fucking serious about working out. This is not the gym for newbies like me. Not at all.

But he's expecting me, so I put on my big girl panties and enter.

I'm immediately confronted by the smell of sweat and deodorant, and I remember why I eventually canceled my unused gym membership.

I check in at the front desk and give the teen behind the counter the day pass Lach gave me. "I'm a guest," I inform him, redundantly.

He nods. "Sure thing. I'm required to give you a tour of the facility and take down your information before you work out."

I groan. "Seriously? I'm just here to work out with my boyfriend. I don't want a tour."

He shrugs. "Sorry. It's the rules."

And I'm sure this kid has never broken any rule in his life. Yeah, right.

Warm hands reach around me from behind and pull me against a hard chest. Lachlan leans in to kiss my neck. "Hey, babe. Thought you'd bailed on me."

I twist in his arms to face him. "Never. But I gotta say, I'm not impressed. I don't want a sales pitch."

He looks up at the kid behind the counter. "Jimmy, she's with me. If Nick has a problem, have him call me."

I turn my head to smile at the guy. "Yeah, Jimmy. I'm with him."

Jimmy nods. "Sure thing, Mr. Pierce. I'm sure there won't be a problem, though."

Lachlan leads me by hand through the gym of sweaty people doing sweaty things. "I guess your celebrity status pays off," I say.

"All the time." He stops in front of the women's changing room. "I'll meet you out here and we can get started."

Fast-forward thirty minutes later and let's just say that there's a reason I don't dance on stage for hours every night. I'm a wuss with zero stamina. Everything hurts. I'm covered in sweat and am the least sexy I've ever been in my life. I'd better have a six-pack and thighs of fucking steel by morning or I'm suing.

Lachlan is telling me to do another set of pushups. I flip him off. "I'm done. I won't be able to walk tomorrow and that sacrifice will be for all the wrong reasons."

He laughs. "It can't be that bad. I went easy on you."

"Easy? You've killed every muscle in my body. Twice." Fucking reps.

"You have to break muscles down to build them up," he explains for the umpteenth time.

"That's the most fucked up logic I've ever heard. That's not true anywhere else in the known universe, so I'm skeptical it's true here. I think this is one big scam to steal money and sweat from people."

His mouth twitches. "You think gyms are trying to steal sweat?"

I wipe a drop of sweat from my forehead and nod. "Probably the government has found a secret way of powering the world with sweat, and the gyms are secret high-paid distributors of said sweat. It's all a big conspiracy, and I'm not playing into it. No sir!"

Lachlan is laughing hard now. "Oh God, Vi. I love you so much." He leans over and kisses me and all I taste is salt.

"I love you, too, but you're going to need to find a new workout partner. I can't do this."

He reaches for my hand and helps me off the mat. "There's one thing here I think you'll enjoy."

I follow him reluctantly. "If it involves flexing any muscles of any kind for any duration, then no, I won't."

He chuckles. "It doesn't."

Ten minutes later we're soaking in a hot tub and I'm leaning against his chest, his arms around me, a big smile on my face. "Okay, this is my kind of workout."

He kisses my sweaty head. "Can I ask you something?"

"Sure," I say, enjoying the feel of the heat penetrating my sore and tired muscles.

"Now that I've decided to stay despite losing my funding, I need to rethink my plans for the youth center, but I'm having a hard time. I've had such a particular vision in my head for so long, I can't imagine anything else."

I stroke his arm as I think about it. "It makes sense that it's hard to shift gears. Why not start from the basics? What do you, at the core, want out of this venture? What are you trying to accomplish?"

He's silent for a moment before speaking. "I want kids in this area to have a safe place to come after-school to study, learn, and dance. I want to teach those who are interested how to take their dance to the next level so they have a way out of their lives, should they need one."

"That's good," she says. "So what do you absolutely need to make that happen? Not what you want or think would be cool. But what do you really *need*?"

"A space. Primarily we need a space for the kids to come, for dance lessons to happen, for studying and after-school classes to take place. And I'd need at least a few people other than myself there to help run it and teach."

"So that's what you look for. Look for that space. Not the space in your head, but the space that will actually work. And then think of ways to generate funding for it. You've been looking for an investor or two. Have you considered letting the kids use their skills to raise the funds through a large group of interested people in the community? A fundraiser of some kind?"

Lach's arms tighten around me. "A fundraiser..." he trails off. And for the first time since he lost his funding, I hear a smile in his voice as he starts talking about plans for the center.

TWENTY SIX

Lach

I have an idea. A grand idea of helping kids and teaching dance. And the idea is great, but it's time to think smaller. Think about what I *really* need to accomplish. Marvin was right. I got stuck on one way of doing things. The Spacey Mall. Investors. I need to be open to other possibilities. The fundraiser is the first step.

Vi and I toss around ideas for how to organize it as we walk back to the car, our sweat-covered bodies glistening in the sun. "Kacie and Tate can invite some of their clients," she says.

I nod. "And we can make posters. I'm sure Kevin and his friends will help pass them out."

"I could hang some up in the store."

I raise an eyebrow. "Advertising a youth fundraiser alongside purple dildos?"

She shrugs. "Lots of my customers have kids."

We pass the closed-down building I noticed earlier. An old man with a long gray beard walks out the door, a brown box under his arm, and locks up. I've never seen anyone in the place. Makes me curious. "Excuse me. Is this your gym?"

The man grunts. "Used to be. Couldn't keep up with the rent. Not with that other gym across the block." He shakes his head. "Should have opened somewhere far away from competition."

Poor guy. I imagine having to close down the youth center. It would break me. "I'm sorry you had to close down."

He rubs his eyes and hiccups. "Yeah, me too. We had a nice family place, you know. A place where the kids could play while you and your honey got a workout in. Close to the schools. I'll miss it." Another hiccup. "Well, see ya." He grunts again and wanders down the street, wobbling side to side. I wonder if there's a bottle of whiskey in his box. I'd be drowning my sorrows too if my dreams collapsed.

I examine the closed gym. It's in nice condition. Looks spacious through the windows. The place must have been great.

And it could be again.

I spin on Vi, startling her. "I have an idea," I say, barely able to contain my excitement. "This could be the place. For the youth center."

Her eyes light up. "It's perfect. And if it's close to schools, that means a shorter drive for parents."

"Exactly." My mind runs with ideas. "I'll contact the schools, see if they're interested in the fundraiser."

"Yes, we can give them posters."

"Yes!"

Vi raises her hand and I high-five her, because you know, we're cool like that. We rush back home, shower, and get to work. Vi contacts Kacie and Tate and starts work on the posters, googling Photoshop tutorials. I call nearby schools, explaining the fundraiser. I manage to reach one of the principals, a woman with a high-pitched voice, and she sounds very interested. "We'll send forms home with the kids. I know a lot of parents who will love this." I thank her and move on to the next school on my list. Not everyone is as responsive. It's okay. I'm making progress, and it feels fantastic.

I contact the owner of the closed gym and talk price. He stutters through the whole conversation. I can tell he's desperate to rent but trying not to show it. In the end, I offer to buy the building outright. "That's...that's a nice offer."

I chuckle. It's nothing compared to what the Spacey Mall would have cost. "You want it, or not?"

"I...um...yes...I want it. I want it."

"Good. Let's meet tomorrow and finalize the deal." We arrange a time to meet at the gym.

Vi glances at me, still sitting on the couch with her laptop. "That's pricey."

It is, which is why I've decided something else. I call my real estate agent, Lucy. "I want to pull out of escrow."

She pauses. "Let's meet and talk about it."

"Sure." I set a time for the next day, before my meeting with the gym owner.

Vi taps on her keyboard. "I thought you loved that house."

"I did, but I don't need it right now. The next house I buy, I want to buy with you."

Her cheeks flush happily and she continues making the poster. We work late into the night and fall asleep on the floor. The next day, I meet with Lucy at her office. Her assistant, a petite redhead, brings us tea. Lucy sits cross-legged on a couch, her short blond cut in an A-line. "So, what made you change your mind?"

I sip the tea. It's bitter and hot. "I'm simplifying. Focusing on what's important."

She fidgets with her fingers. "But you loved that house. You told me you dreamed of having one like it since you were a kid."

"I did. But I have other dreams now."

She sighs. "You're a pain in the ass, you know that?"

I grin. "I make up for it in other ways."

She puts her tea down on the desk and flips through a folder. "You may have to pay fees."

"It's worth it."

She pinches her lips. "Anything I can say to change your mind?"

"Nope." I take another sip of tea. "But when I'm ready to buy, I hope you can be my agent."

That seems to put her at ease. "Of course." We conclude our business, and she starts making phone calls.

Next, I meet the owner at the gym and inspect the property. Some of the wallpaper is peeling, but otherwise it's in good shape. We barter on the price. I manage to save a grand based on the damages. The owner shakes my hand. "I'll send you the paperwork." He looks relieved the deal is almost over.

"Looking forward to it."

As the sun starts setting, I leave the gym, drop by a store, and drive to Kevin's. He's sitting on the sidewalk again, tossing his tennis ball. I hand him a new board, decorated in red and purple grunge art.

His hands shake as he takes it. "Dude, I said I didn't want a free board." By the excited look in his eyes, though, I can tell he doesn't really mean it.

"Good. Because I need your help."

His eyes stay on the board. "What do you need?"

"I'm putting on a fundraiser for the youth center. I need you and your friends to put on a show."

"You mean you need us to impress those suits?"

I grasp his shoulder. "Sure do. Think you can help me out, buddy?"

He finally looks away from the board and into my eyes. "No problem, Lach. I'll tell my friends. We'll make it happen."

"Thanks, dude." I pat him on the back, and we walk up the porch and into the house. Mary's sitting at the kitchen table, her face in her hands She leans her head back, noticing us. "Oh—hi, boys. Didn't hear you coming." Her eyes are red. She's been crying.

I sit down across from her. "What happened?"

"I just had a hard day, is all."

We don't talk of troubles. But when those troubles make my friend cry, I want to hear them. I want to help. "Mary, family doesn't knock. But you know what family does? Family helps each other."

She blows her nose into a napkin, then shakes her head rapidly. "You're right. So, I'll tell you. Bill fired me. Said a younger waitress would bring in more tips. Said I was too old." Her words turn into sobs. "I want to look younger, Lachlan. Why can't I look younger?"

I grab her hands and hold them gently. "You've had a hard life, Mary. I've known people who, in your position, would have lost themselves in a bottle years ago, would have given up on their kid. You haven't. Be proud of that. Be proud of who you are."

The sobs continue, but she smiles through them. "Thank you, my boy. Thank you."

I relax in my chair and grin. "Besides, I don't know what Bill's talking about. You're crying and you still look beautiful."

"Oh, shut it." Her cheeks grow redder. She may just be blushing. "Go on, now. I need to look up jobs tonight."

"I've got something," I say. "I've made progress on the center." And saved some money by pulling out of escrow. "Now I need a secretary."

She waves her hand dismissively. "I can't do that."

"Sure you can. Better than me, that's for sure."

She pauses and finally looks up from her hands. A small smile creeps in at the corners of her mouth. "Well, I suppose I can take the job." She tries to act casual, but I can see the hope flicker in her eyes and can tell this is a big deal for her. "Thank you, Lachlan."

I'll make sure she never has to wear high heels again.

Kevin groans in the corner. "Lach, you mean mom's gonna be at the center *every day?*"

Mary and I chuckle. I say goodbye, promising to drop by soon to discuss the details of her new job. She grins excitedly, all pretenses gone in the face of this new opportunity.

On the way home, I drive by Bill's Burger. The open sign is flickering. I've had to keep my distance in the past, for Mary's sake.

Not any fucking more.

I park and jump out of the car, slamming the doors open as I enter the restaurant. A teenage couple sits in the corner. The place has a foul odor, like week-old meat. "Bill. Where the fuck are you, Bill?"

A man speedwalks out from the back, mustard stains on his red shirt, his eyebrows thick and bushy. "What the hell's goin—"

I grab his hand, twist it behind his back, and slam him facedown into a table. "What's going on, Bill, is your epiphany. You're about to realize that it's time to start treating your employees with respect. You're about to realize that there's consequences for being a dickwad. You following, Bill?"

Bill's breath hitches, and I can feel the fight deflate out of him. "Uh-huh."

"Good. So, I'm going to let you go, and you'll rise a changed man. A respectful man. And if you ever revert to your dark ways, I'll be back. And if you ever even *think* of reporting this..." I squeeze his shoulder until he yelps. "...Just remember how many health codes this place has violated." I knock his head against the table one more time and let go. I stride out, glowing with pride. Man, today has been productive.

Shit's getting done, bitches.

TWENTY SEVEN

Vi

The fundraiser is being held at a local high school gym. The kids did an amazing job of transforming the space into a very fancy ballroom, and this is a black tie affair. I look around and see Kacie and Tate scrambling to get last-minute decorations in place. They offered Hitched to help Lachlan cater and run the event, and he accepted with a grateful heart. Kacie said they could always write it off as a charity event when I asked if she was sure.

And Sebastian has invited everyone he knows with ties and money.

Tonight, the kids will perform something they'd been working on for a while, and then we'll all hope that the raw talent and enthusiasm will attract donors to make their dreams happen.

Lachlan looks amazing tonight in his tux. He kisses me and squeezes my hand. "I have to go get the kids ready. Thank you, babe, for this. For everything."

I pull him close. "Thank *you* for staying and still finding a way to make this happen," I whisper. Because I couldn't stand him leaving. I would have supported him in it, if that's what he needed to do. But it would have broken my heart.

Instead, my heart is swelling in my chest, filling me with a glorious happiness I didn't know existed and never knew could be so strong.

The auditorium is filling with bigwigs from all sectors of life in Vegas. There are doctors, lawyers, investors, performers... I even see the famous magician Kacie's friends with. He helped Kacie win Sebastian back when she almost blew it with Dr. Sexy.

But tonight isn't about us. It's about Lachlan and the kids he's trying to help. Tonight *has* to be a success. I close my eyes, cross my fingers, and send the kids all the luck I can muster.

As lights flash, Lachlan takes the makeshift stage. His deep accent fills the room. "Good evening, and thank you so much for joining us tonight. These kids have worked hard to put together a show we believe you will really enjoy. It's our hope that when you see what they can do, you'll also see why an after-school program is so important in this community, and how deserving these amazing kids are." He pauses and smiles, his pride in the kids beaming across the room. "So without further ado, I'll hand the floor over to them."

Lights go out and someone taps my shoulder. My parents! I hug them both and whisper, "What are you doing here?"

"We just drove in. We couldn't miss your man's big night. We're here to support," my mom says. "We even got a few donations from some friends in California to help out."

My eyes fill with tears, and I know Lachlan will be deeply touched by their presence. He doesn't talk much about it, but I can tell he misses having a parental unit in his life.

The kids take the stage, and I'm nervous for them. I've never seen them dance and have no idea what to expect. What if they blow it and the crowd leaves disappointed with their wallets intact? All of them would be devastated. Lachlan most of all. I narrow my eyes and personally vow to tackle anyone who tries to leave without contributing.

But my fears are in vain, I realize, as soon as the music starts. Because these kids are seriously amazing. Like, unbelievable. They must have dance in their DNA to pull off some of the moves they do.

After the first song, it's clear the crowd is won over. I spy some people already pulling out checkbooks. A very good sign indeed.

By the end, we are all breathless with the talent that exists in these youths. I can see why Lachlan loves working with them so much.

I want to run to him and kiss and hug him and congratulate him, but he takes the stage once more and surprises us all with a last piece. "This one is for a special woman who has changed my life. Vi, I love you."

My heart explodes in my chest as a spotlight lands on me while Lachlan removes his jacket and takes the stage with the boys. And then he dances and the crowd goes wild and my heart is knocking against my ribs like a wild animal and I can't even contain the amazement I feel.

At the end, they all grab signs from the back and, in one fluid movement, turn to reveal what they are holding. After a beat, all eyes are on me.

The signs read, "Vi, will you marry me?"

Lachlan walks over to me and holds out a small black box with a sparkling diamond ring in it. "I don't want to spend another day of my life without you," he says.

Tears stream down my face, tears I didn't even know were flowing, and I run into his arms and the crowd cheers and whistles. "Yes! Yes, I will marry you. Forever, yes!"

TWENTY EIGHT

Lach

Everything is changing.

And I couldn't be happier.

Tonight is my last night as the lead dancer in the Aussie Posse. I've been with these guys for so many years I've lost count. It's crazy to think it's ending after this show.

Vi is in the audience with Kacie, Sebastian, Zoe—even Tate. He and I have hung out a few times and become friends. Slow and steady. We can't turn on the BFF spout quite like the women in our lives.

Still, I was surprised when Vi said he would be here. I thought the first time had traumatized him enough.

I put on the show of my life. I think of Vi the whole time and dance as if she is the only one in the room. Of course she's the woman I pick for my on-stage lap dance. I'm not an idiot, and I'm sure as fuck not going to thrust my groin into another woman's face with my fiancé in the audience.

The guys rib me about it, but fuck them. I get to spend the rest of my life with this woman.

The lights are hot. The dancing is hotter. The crowd is on fucking fire. I close with a flourish of flips and hip-thrust to a standing ovation.

Staring into the glare of white lights, I silently bid goodbye to this chapter of my life. I won't miss it, but I'll always remember it fondly.

The guys slap me on the back as I head to my dressing room. I'm ready to get out and get with Vi. But when I come out, she's already waiting for me with an impish grin on her beautiful face. "Come with me, lover boy."

I grasp her hand and follow. "What's going on?"

"You'll see. By the way, you were amazing tonight. You'll have to fuck me later just to scratch the itch you put inside me with that performance."

I grin and give a half bow as we walk. "Your wish is my command."

When we get to the main dressing room, there's a big cake in the middle of a table, a whole lot of booze, and all the guys plus Vi's friends waiting for me.

Darrel walks over and hugs me. "I'm gonna miss you, Lach, but I'm proud of you. I know we've had some ups and downs over the years, but working with you was always more than just work. You're like a son to me and I'm proud of you."

His words choke me up. "Thanks. That means a lot to me. You know, the fundraiser we had for the center was a hit. We got the funding we needed to open the center and staff it. If you ever feel like a career change, we could use some more dance teachers. You taught me everything you know."

He smiles. "If I ever do, I'll call you." He grows serious. "But, Lach. I may have taught you everything *I* know, but I didn't teach you everything *you* know. You are a prime example of the student surpassing the teacher. Go pass that on to some punk-ass kids like yourself. The world of dance—hell, the world in general—will be better for it."

He walks away, not one for long goodbyes, and Duke comes over and fist bumps me. "Good show, dude. Hard shoes to fill."

"You'll kill it," I tell him.

"And hey. I'm sorry what I said about your woman. It was a dick move and I shouldn't have."

"We're cool, man," I say. "Stay sharp out there. The guys need you."

Vi brings me a glass of champagne and I sip it and smile at her. "Did you know about this?"

"Did you know about my surprise birthday party?" she counters.

"Touché." I kiss her nose. "I love you."

"I love you, too."

We spend a few minutes on our own, talking and kissing, then mingle with the rest. Zoe is being flirted with by one of the guys in the group. Vi cocks her head. "Is he an ass?"

"Larry? Nah, he's a good guy if she's not looking to get serious."

Vi nods. "Okay, good. She's not looking."

Tate is off in a corner making out with one of our groupies. A blond chick I may or may not have banged myself. I nudge Vi. "I thought he was on a fast?"

She laughs. "He got hungry, it would appear."

Kacie and Sebastian come over and shake my hand. "We have to go," Kacie says. "The twins are sick and the babysitter is freaking out."

"Of course," I say. "Thank you for coming. I'm sure we'll see you soon."

Vi hugs her friend and Sebastian and I do the man shake/ hug thing, and they leave.

"Your friends are pretty cool," I tell her.

"They're your friends now too," she says. "More than that. They're family."

For a guy who grew up with none, I'm quickly acquiring a pretty kickass group to call kin. I like it.

. . .

The next day, as Vi and I cuddle and watch a movie together, she fends off texts from her parents and friends. "Everyone's asking about the wedding," she says.

"Tell them we just got engaged. We haven't planned all the details yet."

"I did. They are not accepting that."

I laugh. "Tough shit. It's our wedding."

"I'm thinking summer," she says. "It's plenty of time to get the center off the ground and gives us time to plan a nice event for friends and family without feeling rushed."

I mentally process the time in my head and nod. "Summer sounds great. Maybe the beach? Like your parents? I liked that."

She kisses me, and I take that as a yes.

When the date for the grand opening arrives, I'm a ball of nerves that Vi has to calm. This is it. The day I've been dreaming of. It's finally happening.

Tate and Kacie have been promoting it throughout the city and a lot of people have shown up. Kevin stands beside me with Mary at his back while I give a short speech about what this means to me, to the kids, to this community. Vi is at my side and I'm holding her hand as the crowd cheers and waits for us to cut the giant red ribbon. I give the scissors to Kevin and he looks up in surprise.

"Seriously, man? This is your big moment."

I shake my head. "Nope. It's *ours*. This wouldn't be happening without you. Go ahead."

He is all smiles as he cuts the ribbon and lets the world into The Helping Hand.

People cheer. Angela and Marvin, who drove up from Long Beach just for this, howl and jump up and down in excitement. Sebastian grins, his hands on the baby stroller. Kacie, Tate, and Zoe stand with him. Vi kisses me as people start to pour inside the building. When Mary walks by, she congratulates me. It means a lot.

"You did good, my boy."

"Thank you. I should have passed on that expensive mall a long time ago."

She nods. "I tell you, expensive is not always better. Like with that organic chicken of yours." We all chuckle.

Kevin dashes by his mother. She turns on him. "Excuse me, Kevin McAllister. What did we say about running?"

He shrugs. "Mom, it's a gym. We're supposed to run."

She looks to me. I nod. "Oh, well," she says. "Go ahead then."

Kevin disappears inside the center. I hope he finds a second home here. I hope we all do.

EPILOGUE

Vi

The night of the bachelorette party, I start having doubts. "Do you think this is a good idea?" I ask Kacie.

She glares at me. "The party is in an hour. It no longer matters if it's a good idea or not. After spending weeks on this event, it's happening and you will have fun and that is the last we will say on the matter."

I laugh at her stern face and hug her. "Thank you for doing this. You and Tate are amazing! Do you think it's weird we're combining our parties into one?"

Lachlan and I had talked about this several times and decided we didn't really feel a need for a party with 'the guys' or with 'the girls.' We wanted a big party with all of our friends. After all, one of my best friends is Tate, and I didn't want him excluded just because he has a penis.

So we agreed. A co-ed bachelor/bachelorette party. Which starts soon.

I'm getting ready at Kacie's house and Lach and I will meet at the hotel ballroom that Tate booked for the event. Oh, and did I mention it's a costume party? Because it is. Because who doesn't love dressing up? Lach and I kept our costumes a surprise from each other. Only Kacie and Tate know the truth, and Kacie refuses to give me a hint.

"What if I clash with Lach?" I ask, staring down at my black leather skin-tight cat outfit, complete with a tail and ears. I must admit, I look smokin' hot.

"You won't. Relax."

We say goodbye to Sebastian and the babies and Kacie drives us to the hotel. We're first to arrive and I'm a puddle of nerves, even though this isn't actually my wedding day. But oh my God I'm getting married. MARRIED! It's a bit insane. But I'm excited, because Lachlan is the man for me. I know it in my gut. And I'm so madly in love with him I can hardly stand it.

Kacie and Tate already had the room decorated and so we have very little to do as we wait for the guys.

When Lach and Tate finally show up, my jaw drops. He's dressed as a black panther, with ears, a tail, and a loin cloth, and very little else. His body is rubbed with oils and body paint to give him a sleek look. "Hey, babe. You look amazing."

He kisses me, and if my tail actually worked it would be wagging right now. I purr at him instead and he laughs. "Looks like we have the same mind."

"Looks like."

We're holding hands, grinning like idiots at each other as our friends begin to arrive. Zoe shows up first dressed like an elf, with ears, silver eyes and a silver gown that drapes her petite body. Her hair has been dyed silver to match the dress and her pale skin sparkles with silver glitter. She smiles and though I still see some sadness in her from her breakup with Douche, she's recovering. Regaining her happy.

"Zoe, you are gorgeous. You know, Lach's Aussie Posse are performing tonight. And most of them are single," I tell her with a wink. She could have any single man in this place tonight.

"Ha! We'll see. I'm just here to celebrate you two and have some fun."

The ballroom quickly fills with friends dressed in all manner of costumes. The alcohol flows, music plays, lights flicker over the room in a symphony of color and the joy here is palpable. Lach and I dance all night long, our bodies rubbing together as we kiss and sway to music.

When the Aussie Posse performs, everyone goes wild. Even the guys give a grudging respect to the group. And we threw in a surprise. Two of the female dancers Kacie and Tate employ for parties do a few numbers with the guys, and the resulting performance is sexy, hot and magical.

We don't get home and collapse into bed until the next morning, and I'm very glad we scheduled the actual wedding for Sunday and not today, because I would like to be awake for my wedding.

We sleep most of Saturday, and then I spend the night with Kacie so that we can hold to some silly but fun traditions of waiting to see each other until I walk down the aisle.

The aisle, in this case, is a long golden rug laid between seats set out in the park by a lake. We'd wanted the beach, but we'd also wanted Las Vegas. So the lake it is. It's strewn with red rose petals and leads to an altar with red roses and golden ribbon everywhere. It's stunning, and I feel like a queen when the music plays and I take that first step onto the rug, clutching my father's elbow.

"I'm nervous," I whisper to him, my heart pounding in my chest.

"It's good to be nervous," he says. "You're making a big commitment. But I think it's the right one. I've never seen you so happy, Vi. You glow around him."

"Thanks, Daddy." He actually put on a tux for the event, but I think I spy his Grateful Dead t-shirt peeking out underneath it. I laugh and squeeze his arm. My mom sits in the front row, beaming as I walk down, but my eyes quickly find Lachlan, and then, he's all I see.

When Lach sees me in my golden wedding gown, his eyes light up and his smile dazzles me. I melt a little and lean more on my father until we arrive at the altar.

We say our vows in a blur of nerves and laughter and love, and when we kiss it is magic, and I never want it to end.

As we walk back down the aisle hand in hand, Kacie's final surprise arrives.

It's a hot air balloon with "Just Married" written across it. I laugh and Lachlan smiles, and we board the balloon to the cheers of our friends and family and fly into the brightness of our future together.

THE END

If you enjoyed this book, please take a moment to leave a review online. It's one of the best ways you could help an author, and we'd greatly appreciate it.

Want more sexy? Check out Kacie's story in *Hitched*, and see what happened to your favorite *Whipped* characters.

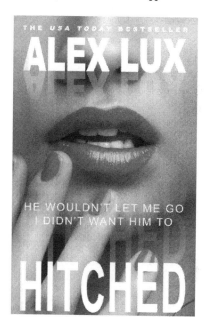

ONE

Unexpected Commitment

"Wife?" I look down at the new ring on my left hand and see a similar ring on him as he stalks toward me in all his glorious nakedness. The water from his recent shower gives his ripped, tan body a sexy sheen.

Our bed is disheveled in a way that only all night fucking can accomplish. Empty bottles of Dom Pérignon litter the high-end hotel room I've unexpectedly woken up in. I've retrieved most of my clothes but stand holding one red high heel; the other is still lost somewhere.

"We appear to have had too much to drink last night," he says with a smirk on his handsome face, cobalt blue eyes penetrating. "I think we both got a bit carried away."

I pull my eyes off his body and focus them on his face, which doesn't help me as much as you might think, because this man is the most gorgeous male specimen I've ever seen in my life, and I work with strippers. Well, okay, mostly I work with women since I own a company that plans bachelor and bachelorette parties, and men are more likely to hire strippers than women. But still, I've seen my share, and this man...I can't even...

With all the intelligence of my Ivy League business degree apparently out to lunch, I repeat again, "Wife?"

He's still naked, by the way, as he moves closer to me and reaches for my left hand. Heat floods me as our skin makes contact. He caresses the gold band on my left hand. "Wife."

His voice is husky and deep, and it sends shivers up my spine as my temporary, alcohol-induced amnesia fades, and a memory from the night before makes a belated appearance at the party.

. . .

I remember him. He was to our right, at a table near the bar, smiling at me with too perfect teeth. My twin brother, Tate, ever the womanizer, nudged me. "I've got my eye on the woman at that table," he said, pointing to a perky blond who was nearly drooling over him. Not that I blamed her. I mean, he's my brother, but I'm not blind. "So you should go for this guy. He's clearly into you."

My best friend, Vi, grinned at me from across the bar, where she'd cozied up to a shy but cute guy that didn't stand a chance against her shapely curves, wild red hair and green eyes. We hadn't been out like this in so long; we'd all been too busy working, building our businesses. Tate works with me at Hitched, and Vi, well…Vi has a unique niche market going in the dominatrix world.

When my brother left me at the bar to woo the panties off the blonde, Mr. Sexy strode over in his suit and tie, exuding confidence, a dark mop of hair offsetting eyes that were an unreal shade of blue. I could tell I was about to have my panties wooed off me as well, and I didn't mind one bit.

"Is this seat taken?" he asked, pointing to where Tate had been sitting.

I smiled. "Not anymore. I think my brother has found someone more exciting to entertain him."

"I find that hard to believe." He slid into the chair, his leg brushing against mine as he pulled in closer.

"Because you know me so well and can with confidence say I'm the most entertaining person here?" I teased, sipping my cocktail.

"I'm good at reading people." He held out his hand, and I took it. "I'm Sebastian Donovan. It's a pleasure to meet you." Instead of shaking my hand, he brought my knuckles to his mouth and, while maintaining eye contact with me, caressed my skin with his lips in a feathery light kiss.

"Kacie Michaels. Nice to meet you," I said as I silently gave my panties notice that they wouldn't be needed for long.

. . .

Other memories are still shadows pulling at my pounding head, trying to break free. "What happened last night?" I ask, still processing the rings. There's no way we tied the knot like drunken assholes in Vegas. Not. Even. Possible.

He hands me some paperwork I hadn't noticed sitting on top of the mahogany dresser. "This happened. I admit to being as surprised as you."

I raise an eyebrow. "I very much doubt that."

His grin falters. "Do you really not remember?"

I look down at the paper. It's a marriage license, signed and stamped and very official looking. Holy shitballs. What the fuck have I done?

"Bits and pieces are coming back," I admit. "But I don't remember this," I say, holding up the paperwork. "This can't be legal."

"I'm afraid it is. I already made a call to my attorney while you were sleeping. Unless you're already married to someone else?" Now he raises his eyebrow, and I scowl.

"I think I'd know if I was previously married."

His lips curve into a sardonic grin, and I sigh at the irony of my own words. "Don't give me that look, dude. This isn't standard operating procedure for me, and I'm guessing—hoping—it's not for you either."

"This is a first," he assures me. "You're the first."

My heart flutters, whether at his words or the way he says them, with heat and desire and all the things that landed me in this spot right now. I know I'm not his first sexual experience. That much is clear. I guess that makes me his first wife. Um, great?

. . .

As the crowd at the bar grew louder, we moved closer to talk. I couldn't help but notice how good he smelled, a spicy, woody scent with hints of cinnamon and cardamom. It made me want to taste him.

As if reading my mind, mid-sentence he leaned in, cupped my face with his hands, and pressed his lips to mine. He tasted like expensive red wine, and he deepened our kiss, exploring my mouth with his, our tongues teasing each other.

When the kiss ended and he pulled away, I felt deflated and aroused all at once. I missed the feel of him, the contact with his body, and a need grew in me that I hadn't felt in quite some time.

He licked his lips and smiled. "I've been wanting to do that since I first saw you walk in with your brother and friend."

I flushed at the thought that he'd been watching me that long. We'd been here for hours.

"You make quite an impression with a first kiss," I said.

"That's just a taste of what's to come." He winked. I nearly swooned. Not actually swooned, because, you know, I'm not a too-tight-corset-wearing damsel from the Victorian era, but if I'd been standing, there'd for sure be some wobbly knees.

This man. He was delicious, and I wanted more.

I plucked the cherry from my drink and sucked on it in a seductive way. "You're not the only one with skills," I said.

He was sitting so close, his knee was between my legs, one hand on my thigh, pushing up the red dress I was wearing. "Shall we go somewhere and explore these skills in more... depth?"

I didn't need to touch him to tell he had enough in his pants to give true depth to those promises. I reached for my purse and caught Tate's eye. He looked at both of us, then smiled and mouthed, "Have fun!"

We walked out of the bar, Sebastian's hand on my lower back, lingering just a little bit too low, fingers exploring the curve of my ass. And I didn't mind a bit. Believe me, if I did, I'd make my thoughts clear. No one has ever accused me of being too shy to express my feelings.

But right now, with this man, there was only one feeling I wanted to express, and it required considerably less clothing.

. . .

"We need to get this annulled," I say, my heart racing. "I mean, that shouldn't be hard. I'm guessing this isn't that uncommon in this city."

He holds eye contact with me, and let me just remind you he is *still naked,* and a part of me wants to lick the water off his body and then reenact the parts of last night I'm starting to remember.

"That would probably be the wisest thing to do," he finally says.

I'm relieved. Obviously. Any other feelings that might be surfacing right now, in light of his easy acquiescence, are of no consequence. I push away that flutter of disappointment and straighten my spine. "Of course it is. We barely know each other."

He apparently knows me better than I know him. My memory is coming back, but slowly. I've never been this drunk before. Well, there was one time, back in college, when I got so drunk I almost did a strip tease on a table, but someone had a video camera, and a friend talked me out of it. I didn't remember anything the next day, but that was my first and only drunk black out. Until now.

Marrying a one-night stand definitely beats stripping on film in my book.

ABOUT ALEX LUX

Alex Lux is a USA TODAY bestselling multi-genre romance author who fancies herself British and living in a swanky flat in London where she and the Queen frequently have tea and crumpets. In reality, she's a native-born Californian who has a great fake accent and often compels her kids to get their fake British on as well. She does love tea, but drinks it with her Sexy Russian Prince (who's not really a prince, but he *is* Russian, and he *is* sexy). Together they write books with lots of sex and intrigue while raising three little girls who are entirely too smart for their parents' own good.

When not penning toe-curling sexiness, she writes fantasy and science fiction with her husband as Karpov Kinrade.

Find her at AlexLuxBooks.com
On Twitter @AlexLuxBooks
On Facebook /AlexLuxBooks
Don't forget to head on over to her website and sign up for her newsletter to receive free books and exclusive giveaways and content just for subscribers!

. . .

If you enjoyed this book, please consider supporting this author by leaving a review wherever you purchased it. Thank you. xx

21855827R00119

Made in the USA
Middletown, DE
12 July 2015